T0207800

THE
GAME
WARDENS

THE GAME WARDENS

BOOK 2
DANGER'S WAY

DAN HAYDEN

THE GAME WARDENS
BOOK 2 DANGER'S WAY

iUniverse books may be ordered through booksellers or by contacting:

iUniverse
1663 Liberty Drive
Bloomington, IN 47403
www.iuniverse.com
1-800-Authors (1-800-288-4677)

Because of the dynamic nature of the Internet, any web addresses or links contained in this book may have changed since publication and may no longer be valid. The views expressed in this work are solely those of the author and do not necessarily reflect the views of the publisher, and the publisher hereby disclaims any responsibility for them.

Any people depicted in stock imagery provided by Thinkstock are models, and such images are being used for illustrative purposes only. Certain stock imagery © Thinkstock.

ISBN: 978-1-5320-2425-2 (sc)
ISBN: 978-1-5320-2426-9 (e)

Library of Congress Control Number: 2017909479

Print information available on the last page.

iUniverse rev. date: 06/19/2017

DEDICATION

This book is dedicated to all the First Responders that routinely respond to and encounter emergency scenarios for the betterment of their fellow man. Police, fire departments, ambulatory services, and environmental protection agencies are but a few of the names worthy of mention. These are the people who continually, and without concern for themselves, consistently risk their own lives so others may survive.

In addition to these unsung heroes, I would like to add Eagle Scout Brian Albert, to the list of these special people, who passed untimely in his young life.

DISCLAIMER

This book is a work of fiction. Names, characters, places and incidents, or incident dates, are products of the author's imagination or are used fictitiously. Any resemblance to actual events or locales or persons, living or dead, is entirely coincidental.

I want no connection with any ship that does not sail fast
for I intend to go in harm's way.

Admiral John Paul Jones

PREFACE

When it concerns anything that might be of a recreational nature, most people tend to forget about all the little essentials that go along with the situation at hand. Instantaneous gratification and emotional need tend to outweigh normal safety considerations which sometimes end in disappointment or fatalities. This is especially true when the event may be something that is of a seasonal nature and the public is overly anxious to get back out there and make their favorite pastime happen.

In the following chapters I have tried to show how the excitement and love for a favorite hobby or sport coupled with the exasperation of a seasonal time constraint can lend itself to a dangerous situation. In the excitement, it is only human nature to just 'get out there' and do it. A good example is a fisherman that has waited for several months for Opening Day and rushes right out to his favorite fishing hole only to forget his bait and in some cases the pole itself. Another example is that of recreational boaters, who in their haste and need to be back on their beloved scow may have forgotten the most important of safety features like Personal flotation Devices (life jackets) or proper attention to the boat and mechanical concerns for the motor.

The recreational devices available to us can allow us to view nature in its most awesome forms and enjoy some of the associated opportunities in the best ways but once taken for granted can be a tool that can easily ruin an otherwise great day or end a life. We have invented these recreational toys to help us enjoy the environment but must remember to pay attention to their capabilities when abused or their rules when neglected.

Dan Hayden
Author, THE GAME WARDENS,
Book 2, Danger's Way
April 2017

CHAPTER 1

It was early on a Monday morning. April had finally arrived and it was time to start preparing for the upcoming boating season. Fishing season would be starting in three weeks and it wouldn't be long before the river became a place of activity, a place where families fished and boated together, where people took long lazy cruises sometimes pulling a water skier, and couples in love found their places along the river banks to picnic and watch birds of all kinds, from ducks to eagles, go through their daily paces. The jet skiers would be back as well as the well-meaning canoeists and kayakers. Yes, the river would be back to serving its people from the town of Thompson as well as from other faraway places.

The concern for water safety would also be there as it was at the start of every new season. Fun and competition on the water always seem to make people become shortsighted on the safety end which means anything goes as long as the fun factor is still present. Ignoring the presence of personal flotation devices (PFDs), otherwise known as life jackets, is a common occurrence among sportsmen and sometimes can prove fatal in the end. Attention to river and weather conditions as well as natural obstructions are important details that seem to require too much thought or concern and is not a favorite part of the recreational process.

Marine Patrol Officer Sam Moody stood at the end of the town boat launch's dock and stared out into the peaceful Connecticut River as he considered these and some of the other marine rules and regulations that boaters and fisherman either don't know, have forgotten or just choose to ignore. The river was a little fast and high, typical for this time of year. It was a mesmerizing site to behold. The moving water was much like watching the flames in a fire. The longer the scene was observed the harder it became to look away from it.

An eagle appeared from upriver, patrolling the east bank. The massive bird never flapped a wing. It just soared toward Sam's position as it scanned the riverbank for prey. Sam just watched the animal as he gazed skyward. *Must be hunting for its morning meal. The female should be by anytime soon to make the actual attack.* The eagle flew over Sam's head and lighted at the top of an old oak just downriver from Sam. As if on cue, the female came into view. She dove toward the water from a much higher altitude above the center of the river. As the male sat and waited, the female targeted a lone black duck that was playfully giving itself a bath on the opposite shore. In one graceful swoop, the female leveled out her dive about twenty feet from the river's surface and made a right turn toward the black duck's position on the opposite shore.

Despite the impending attack, the duck had no inkling that it was being hunted and about to become breakfast. Sam looked over at the male eagle as it sat regally on its perch and watched the show. He smiled. *Just like humans … the man sits and waits while the woman gets the dinner.*

The female dropped its altitude slowly as it honed in on the unsuspecting duck. About twenty feet from its prey, the female was skimming the surface of the water with its talons extended forward in a reaching fashion. Suddenly the black duck upended and dove under the river's surface. In an instant the female's talons touched the water where the duck had submerged, lifted its own huge body and swooped upward and around in an almost one hundred eighty degree turn to miss the low overhang of trees on shore. Sam grabbed his binoculars and scanned the river's surface for the duck. Then he saw it surface closer to shore but farther underneath the safety of the overhanging limbs of trees that bordered the river bank. The duck had been clever and knew it could swim underwater to the safety of the low overhang. Gaining altitude as she flew back out toward the middle of the river, the hunting female suddenly made a quick diving turn back toward the duck, talons extended, and this time tried to make a sideway grab for its prey. The turn was so tight and low one of the eagle's wingtips splashed the water. Once again, the duck dove under the safety of the river's surface just as the eagle's talons skimmed its head. Banking hard, the eagle did some fancy, evasive flying to avoid a collision with more tree branches that extended out over the river's surface. Sam watched the hunt with amazement. *Circle of life,* he thought. *Each has to do what it takes to survive-no good guys, no bad guys.* Then he smiled to himself. *Duck two-Eagle zero.*

Sam kept his binoculars trained on the section of water where he figured the duck would surface. Finally, the duck's head popped up, this time closer to shore. The eagle repeated its maneuver once again and made a halfhearted attempt toward the duck. The eagle banked to the right and upward instead of going in under the trees. The female flew back across the river toward the waiting male, in a defeated retreat, banked again as she flew by his perch as if to say, 'We're leaving. Get your own breakfast,' and headed back upriver by herself. Sam watched the male as it stared at its departing mate. Finally, the male flew off and followed the female. Sam smiled and shook his head as he said aloud to himself. "Not much different from human behavior," and began getting the Carolina ready for the morning's patrol.

Sam went through all the necessary checks before leaving the dock. Since he was by himself he double checked some of the more important items. The first thing he did was check on all the safety equipment. PFDs, throwables (throwable life jackets), oars, extra line, anchors, first aid kit … all there. Then he reached up over the helm and opened the radio box. He turned on all the onboard electronics and police radio. Next, he tipped the 40 horsepower Honda engine down into the water by thumbing a knob on the throttle, switched on the ignition and choked the engine. As he looked to the stern, Sam glanced at the engine's lower end. Water spit out of the engine cowling. *Good flow,* Sam thought. He scanned the dashboard in front of him … all gauges and dials responding … batteries (batts) good, depth sounder ON, engine RPM normal, oil good. In a muffled but audible tone Sam said aloud, "Okay, Ready to go," and threw on his life jacket.

With the engine settling into a steady and rhythmic idle, Sam released the deck lines-first the bow, then the stern. The boat was already downstream of the river's current and started to move away from the dock. "Here we go," Sam said as he gently nudged the throttle forward. The Carolina responded and the patrol boat obediently moved away from the dock. Sam snatched the radio's microphone (mic) from the radio box and keyed it to identify himself and the Carolina to Dispatch. "Headquarters from 419. Marine one is underway and on patrol heading north, Connecticut River." "Roger 419," came the curt reply from Dispatch. *Think I'll head for the Mass line* (Massachusetts border) *first and see what's happening up river. There has got to be someone up there doing something.* He turned the helm over to starboard and the Carolina headed upriver against a moderate current.

The first thing Sam had to do was get the boat into the river's channel. This was always a challenge because of its position in the river and the narrow width it allowed for a boat to pass. The old piers that once supported the iron truss bridge and carried vehicles for trade and commerce to and from Thompson were the only remnants that remained of the one hundred year old structure.

The Carolina approached the first pier, closest to Thompson's shoreline and Sam skillfully maneuvered around it making sure to keep a distance from the dangerous back eddies and whirlpools caused by its position in the current. Once past, he maneuvered the Carolina into a position so the boat's stern was in line with the pier and the bow pointed at a lone power stanchion two miles ahead that marked the state line between Massachusetts and Connecticut.

As the Carolina started up river Sam decided the current felt a little heavy so he kept a moderate amount of throttle applied otherwise the patrol boat would lose forward momentum or 'way' as marine officers called it. He didn't want to approach the channel with too much speed because he knew he'd have to back the throttle down and slow the boat just before he entered the ledge area. Hitting the channel entrance too fast usually meant the lowest part of the engine cowling, just beneath the propeller (prop) called the skeg, had a good chance of hitting a loose rock on the river bottom.

Immediately the depth sounder alarm began to moan. The Carolina was approaching the ledge. *Here we go*, thought Sam. *Six feet right down to two feet ... got to watch it here.* Sam still let the prop ride at its normal cruising depth. He knew he could also loose way if he tipped up the engine too much with this much current. *Just keep an eye on that stanchion up river and the depth sounder display … should be alright if I stay in the middle of this so-called channel.* Sam had to continually keep correcting his course. He swung the helm to port then immediately to starboard. The wind had also increased the amount of chop (waves) in the water which wasn't helping the situation. The depth sounder went off again causing Sam to glance at its display. "Shit … one foot six," Sam said to himself. He fingered the engine tilt drive (tip switch) on the throttle with his right thumb and gave it a gentle stab. Obediently, the prop tipped up and away from the channel's rocky bottom a few inches. Sam looked ahead and saw the bow was not lining up with the power stanchion a mile ahead, "Drifting to port," he murmured. With that, he goosed the throttle a smidge and the Carolina picked up a little speed. The depth sounder went silent and the bottom went to two foot six. Sam thumbed the tip switch and brought the prop back down to regular cruise depth.

The game of good water/bad water went on and on until Sam spotted the end of the ledge area, marked by a red house that sat on the river's west bank atop a small rise. It was a welcome landmark that all sailors passing this area were happy to see. Just as the Carolina got abeam of the red house, the depth sounder read two foot four then immediately to six feet. Sam smiled to himself, took in a deep breath and shoved the throttle forward to three-quarters AHEAD. The Carolina's bow lifted into the air as she responded to the increased RPMs and then flattened out with the increased speed. The patrol boat was now on plane and skipping across the wave tops. Sam opened her all the way up to full AHEAD and the patrol boat headed for the Massachusetts state line. *There's the peninsula*, he thought. The wind blew through the Carolina's deck space. Even though Sam was protected by the center console and wind screen, he always turned his baseball style Class B hat backward with the bill facing the rear so it wouldn't fly off. The Bimini top over Sam's head also helped to channel the air blowing by. Still, it was a bumpy ride.

As Sam approached the peninsula he gave the beach and camping area a quick glance over his starboard (right) side. Nothing … no fishermen, no beached boats, no campers. Sam smiled to himself feeling as if this might be a quiet day on the river. As he passed the midpoint of the peninsula, he brought the engine throttle back to mid–range. The boat slowed to approximately 20 knots. He didn't want to be going too fast as he approached the state line because he planned on doing a long sweeping port (left) turn into Massachusetts water, make a 180 (a complete turn back in the original direction of travel), and return to Connecticut water again. There was also a speed limit on this river and since there was no emergency, didn't want to abuse the regulation.

Fifty yards ahead lay the power lines that crossed over the river. They were positioned about two hundred feet above water level and were marked with large orange balls attached to their guy wires every one hundred foot of length. Those lines were the agreed on landmark by both Border States for a visual view of the state line. Sam began his turn to port. The boat didn't slip to the side at this speed although he was watching for it. Sam was just running her through the paces to get her feel again after a long winter. The Carolina was handling perfectly. As soon as Sam crossed back into Connecticut water he slowed the boat gradually and finally brought the engine throttle almost all the way back to NEUTRAL. The stern wave caused by his forward momentum came up to meet the still moving Carolina and rolled under her from stern to bow giving the rider a rolling sensation. Once the wave passed, Sam left the engine idling and drifted under the power lines. Now that the boat was almost dead in the water he noticed the wind that had caused the chop and steerage difficulties while navigating the channel, was gone. Remembering back, that was one of the river fairway's characteristics. The wind could be blowing hard one minute in one part of the river and be almost non-existent in another.

Sam reached for the ignition key and switched it off. The Carolina was now dormant. The only sound was the creaking of the boat as it rocked with the current passing underneath. Some water noises could be heard as the larger chop splashed against the patrol boat's sides. Sam looked into the water and thought the current was less in this area, and naturally so, because this part of the river was very wide and much deeper than down river. He decided to just let the boat drift for a while. The boat was in the middle of the river and further north of where they practiced river extraction practice last year. It would be calm enough for the time being.

Sam sat down on the skipper's bench seat and looked to the open sky. It was a beautiful day with sun and no clouds. He closed his eyes and just let the sun's rays warm his upturned face. With his eyes still closed he could hear the distant call of a hunting hawk somewhere high above the river. Just the sounds around him were present and seemed to envelope him and the Carolina as it drifted on the water. Sam began to relax. He could feel the boat under him sliding downriver with what current there was in this area, but still, it was slow and comfortable. Sam opened his eyes and dropped his gaze to the deck. Just then a large splash happened off the starboard side. Sam quickly looked right to see a full size adult Carp of about three feet long, jump free of the water, clearing its entire body length from the water. He didn't know if it had snatched an unsuspecting bug from the air or just jumped, as that particular fish was sometimes known to do. The carp seemed to turn on its side and fall back into the water making another large splash. Sam began to enjoy the morning. *This is what it's all about*, he thought. *These are nature's gifts for everyone to enjoy. This is a beautiful place. I should consider myself lucky I've been reassigned to river patrol.* The thought gave way to more deep thinking and then he began to consider what had actually caused his reassignment. Sam went back through the whole scenario of last fall's firefight in New Hampshire and how he had violated the rules of jurisdiction as a Connecticut State Game Warden. Thank god he had requested Special Police Powers. That was probably the only thing that saved his job.

Sam glanced up at the west shoreline now and then to ensure he was still a safe distance from shore. He noticed the boat was following the main current and was drifting toward the west side. He was still okay and had plenty of deep water here. *Think I'll just let her drift a while more. There's no boat traffic and the water is a lot calmer here. It'll kill some time before I have to head back to the boat ramp.* Sam went back to considering his plight. Meanwhile the Carolina slipped further and further down river.

He continued to let his thoughts wander. Lieutenant Alban, the Unit Commander, was still treating him as an outsider and barely gave him the time of day when he did report to headquarters for a meeting or special request. His buddies and partners in crime regarding the New Hampshire incident, Tom Stafford and Pat James were both on nights but still at their originally assigned posts. Everyone involved had been suspended without pay for different durations but only Tom and Sam had been busted in rank. The brass had seen to it that for further punishment Tom and Pat would be assigned to the grave yard shift indefinitely. Sam's thoughts continued to ponder the situation. He no longer felt the guilt he had experienced after the court case. The three officers had talked all that out on Thompson's West Hills cliffs one Sunday afternoon. Everyone was healing and moving on with their lives and careers. Suddenly, he felt a sudden stab at his heart's core. *Where has Lee been all this time?* Maybe he should have called him and asked if he was okay. Sam didn't know what he should do about it. Lee didn't have a phone so he couldn't just call him up. Maybe it was time for another hike up to the High Meadow for a talk with the tracker and sportsman guide. Then Jake Farmer's memory took the stage in Sam's mind. It was unfortunate about the warden turned poacher and his extended stay in the hospital but that man didn't deserve an easy solution for his predicament or any forgiveness either. Finally, Sam's thoughts landed on Helen Woodruff. What will become of her? A sweet, middle-aged widow that had been used in the worst way … and now relegated to live out the rest of her days with what Jake had done to her and how he had used her good intentions.

Suddenly, the boat lurched a little snapping Sam out of his daydreaming. He looked up to see the boat was getting near the faster water. He panned the river and noticed the boat was approaching the area where rookie Steve Hanks was murdered. Sam stood up from the skipper's bench seat. *There's the spot,* Sam thought. Sam let the Carolina drift a little closer, then went to the bow and threw out one of the bow anchors, let the line pay out a little, pulled it taut and secured it to a line cleat on the Carolina's gunnel.

Sam sat back down and looked out over the water where the previous year's boat tragedy had occurred. He just stared blankly, without thinking, for a while. Finally, he pulled his gaze from the water and looked up river seeing the same open stretch of water Hank's killer had seen when he escaped the scene that fateful night. The killer's view would have been the same except for the fact it had happened at night. The open stretch of water upstream would have been dark black outlined by grey walls of trees on either side of the river, like an unlit hallway.

Sam looked back into the water thinking how the Carolina had been rafted up to a suspect boat of the Checkmate class, bow to stern, and how he and Hanks were holding the two vessels together so Lieutenant Alban could talk to the people in the Checkmate. He remembered how Alban had tried to board and then all hell broke loose. The next thing he knew, Hanks was lying dead in the water and Alban lay in a prone position starboard to port side, unconscious. The Avon was slowly sinking because of a collapsed air chamber caused by the collision with the Carolina … Suddenly Sam stood up from the bench seat and said aloud, "Those bastards! They got Hanks and they think they got away with it. Those bastards!" Sam had just had a revelation. Everything was falling into place now. "I'm going to make this assignment work for me … and Hanks. I'll use this new assignment to find that Checkmate and the guys that were in it." Sam felt a new exhilaration run through his body … one he hadn't felt in a long time. He looked up river and smiled. Then he said, "Everything happens for a reason. That's why I'm here. I am the River Patrol now and I am going to get those guys." He paused a moment then said in a softer tone, "I told you we'd do you right, Steve. We'll get 'em."

★ ★ ★ ★

CHAPTER 2

Sam returned to his cabin after a long day on the river. He found it hard to concentrate on anything else after his revelation earlier in the day about hunting down Steve Hanks' killer. He spent the rest of the day entertaining different ideas, who he would ask to get involved, and how he was going to approach the new idea. He had barely said a word to his wife Peg at dinner and she knew something was on his mind. Peg had tried to get him to talk but he merely offered one or two word answers. She was trying to avoid another scenario like the New Hampshire one and wanted him to come forward on his own and offer the sacred information. Finally, Sam stood from the dinner table, "I'm going to sit by the fire a while. Got some thinking to do." Peg just nodded at him and began to wonder if he was returning to the old Secret Sam-keeping things from her that she should be aware of. She just nodded and said, "I'll be in after I clean up here, if you want to talk about it."

Sam only heard that she may join him in front of the fire as he pushed his chair in and headed off for the living room where his big easy chair waited in front of the fire place hearth. Sam dropped into the chair and stared into the flames and felt his whole being start to relax. There is something about a fire that seems to entrance the person staring into it … just as the rippling water had done earlier in the day as he drifted downriver. *Where do I start,* he thought. *I should probably go all the way back to the night of Hanks' death. We all sort of put it out of our minds because of all that was going on but it's high time the situation is addressed. Do I talk to Marine Sergeant Smalls? He spent a good portion of that summer looking for those guys with double patrols until Alban told him to back off. Said he didn't find anything though … maybe I'll just kind of hint around at it. See if he did uncover anything. Don't want to let on that I'm going after those guys … at least not yet. I'll see him at roll call in the morning.*

Peg walked into the room and sat on the arm of Sam's chair and laid her closest arm over Sam's shoulders. She caressed the hairline at the back of his neck with her fingers. "What is so heavy on your mind, Sam? You need to discuss these things with me … remember?" Sam kept his eyes on the fire and barely felt the fingers on his neck. "Yeah, I know. Right now I'm just kicking around an idea I came up with while I was drifting around in the boat today." Peg smiled, "Well, what was it? Maybe I can help." Sam paused a while then said, "I drifted into the area where Hanks was murdered two years ago. I dropped anchor and just sat there thinking about what happened and how it happened … so unnecessary." Sam stopped and continued staring into the fire. Peg was relieved that he was beginning to discuss the problem he had been considering. " … And," Peg left the question open. Sam just blurted it out, "I want to hunt down Hanks' killer. He's still out there and he thinks he got away with it." Peg stood up from the chair and faced Sam, "Are you serious? Why does it have to be you that go after all the extra unsolved problems? New Hampshire is still fresh in everyone's mind and you're still on thin ice with the PD's administration." "Peg, I'm in a perfect position to investigate this. All I'm going to do for now is keep my eyes open, ask some questions, maybe go back and read back over the incident file for that night to see if there's anything anybody missed." She stood and stared at her husband. Sam returned the look with an expression that said he was going to do it anyway. Peg put her hands on her hips, "Sam?" He reached for her hand and gently took it in his, "I'll keep you informed, Honey. No hero stuff this time … don't worry." Peg glared at him a few seconds longer, "Uh huh," and left the room. Sam watched her leave. *At least I told her what I was thinking … didn't expect her to like it.*

The next morning's roll call came all too soon. Sam was early and entered the locker room to find the guys getting ready for the morning shift. "Hey," someone shouted, "it's Waterdog!" Sam threw a towel at the playful warden and whispered in his ear, "Better hope you never have to ride with me. It'll be a long day for you." Then he walked to the end of the row and stood leaning against the wall where Tom Stafford and Pat James were. They looked up at Sam as they finished dressing, "Hey Buddy," Stafford stood up and nudged Sam with an open hand to the chest. Pat just nodded. Sam stared at the two a moment, then said, "I need to talk to you guys in the cafe after roll call. Tom and Pat looked at each other then nodded their heads but in their own minds knew something was brewing.

Roll call was typical and routine. Just the usual, 'today pay attention to people fishing in state stocked streams, ponds, and lakes before opening day' lecture, and 'be ready to assist marine patrol' in the event of any pre-season boating accidents. Hunting season, for the most part was over and small game hunting season was coming to a close. All the attention was starting to shift toward the Marine Division. Lieutenant Alban, still cool toward Sam, made a feeble attempt at the end of roll call to include him as part of the group. "Officer Moody … Sergeant Smalls couldn't attend roll call this morning due to an early morning incident. Please make sure you get with him and ensure the Carolina as well as the Avon are up to snuff. I want entire system checks completed by this weekend, tune-ups … the works. Can't afford to have one of those boats down, especially this time of the year. It's striped bass season and there's going to be striped bass fishermen on the river this week looking for an early catch, and it's legal since the Connecticut is open all year around." Moody nodded, "Okay, LT."

Moody, Stafford and James sat in their usual corner in the back of the room. When the lieutenant dismissed the group they all stood as Alban left the room. Stafford turned toward Moody and asked, "What's on your mind, Sam," a look of concern was evident on Stafford's face. "Let's go to the cafeteria to discuss it." Noticing Stafford's demeanor Sam added, "Don't look so concerned. It's just an idea I came up with yesterday." Stafford grinned and said, "That's what I'm worried about."

The three old friends sat in a far corner of the cafeteria while Sam informed the other two of his idea to hunt down Hanks' killer. A half serious Tom Stafford responded rather loudly to Sam's new idea, "Ahh, Sam … for Pete's sake. We just got through one of your ordeals and now it looks like we're heading right into another one. Isn't anything ever routine for you?" Sam just calmly eyed Stafford. "You don't have to partake if you don't feel inclined. I'm not asking for your help. I'm just running it by the two of you." Pat James spoke up, "Yeah, buddy. You know damn well that we wouldn't let you do any of that serious stuff by yourself." Sam just smiled and dropped his gaze to the table. A few awkward moments passed, Stafford took another sip of his coffee, and Pat just let his eyes wander around the cafeteria. Finally, Sam broke the silence, "Well, I'm doing it. You can help if you like but I am going to find those guys. I promised Hanks we'd do him right." "When could you have possibly done that," a curious James stared at Moody. "I stopped by his grave on the way home from the academy on graduation day." Stafford and James both dropped their gaze to the table. "Okay, I'm in," Stafford offered. "Alright, me too then," said James. They all reached out to the center of the table and did their knuckle bump to seal the deal. "What is our first move," asked Stafford. Sam leaned forward, now excited with his friends buy in, "I have to get a look at the incident report for that night without letting Smalls know what I'm up to. If he finds out he'll tell Alban and it'll be over." All three wardens just nodded their heads in agreement. James just shook his head and asked, "Why so secret? Why do we have to keep this from Alban or Smalls?" "We're not keeping it from anyone, Pat. For now, we're just keeping it low key. Things around here are still a little sensitive so I'm taking it slow. If I just go up to Alban with the idea, he's going to dismiss it until things have quieted down completely. Too much exposure in too little a time span. We'll let some time pass while I'm doing the research then I'll mention it to Alban."

Sam paused and looked around the table, "We good?" Everyone nodded in agreement. Sam continued, "I plan on questioning Smalls in a matter of fact sort of way about what he found, if anything, when he was doing double patrols on the river right after the accident." "When are you going to do that," asked Stafford. "He's still out on the river." Sam smiled and said, "After I bring the Carolina in later this afternoon. He's going to be starting the boat checks Alban asked for at the meeting. The checks will be a distraction while I pick his brain." "You do like to walk the edge old buddy. Well, be careful–Smalls is pretty quick. He might be onto you before you realize it." Stafford was concerned. Moody stood up from his chair, "I'll handle it. We'll talk again when I get more information." The three wardens left the cafeteria and went their own ways … Stafford and James to their homes to catch some sleep before shift and Sam headed for the boat house.

★ ★ ★ ★

CHAPTER 3

Marine Sergeant Mike Smalls finished tying up the Carolina at the town boat dock and began walking across the lower parking lot toward his Blazer, Car 3. Sam Moody was at the upper parking lot looking down into the boat launching area and watched the stocky, short tempered marine sergeant approach the wooden staircase to the upper parking lot. Smalls looked up and saw Sam, "Hey, Sam. How was roll call? Anything I should know about?" Smalls just finished one flight of stairs and was beginning to climb the second to where Sam waited. Sam leaned against one of the stair rails and shouted back, "Nah, the usual. Hunting season is over and get ready for the river stuff … fishing season starting, boaters, …you know." Smalls was nearing the middle of the second staircase. Sam added, "LT wants you to have both boats checked out, completed equipment forms, boat status forms, and tune-ups on both boats by Saturday." Smalls stopped climbing the stairs and stood there in utter disbelief. "Are you kidding me? By Saturday? All the shit I have to go through. All those freakin' forms, old equipment, new equipment … and tune ups to boot - Shit! It's Tuesday already and I still have to write about this morning's incident. What's he thinking?"

Moody rolled his eyes and looked out at the river and let Smalls finish his whining. The sergeant still hadn't moved from his place on the stairway. He just stood there verbalizing some expletives and kicked the rail post a couple of times. Finally, Sam looked down at him, "You done, Sarge?" Smalls face was now beat red. "Fuck, I don't have time for all this shit." Smalls started to climb the stairs again. When he reached the top Moody said, "Don't worry, Marine Corporal Sawyer is good with the boat's engines and I'll give him a hand. You take care of the boat and equipment reports, and I'll get all the old gear stowed and tell you what we need for new stuff." Smalls stared at Moody for a brief moment then said, "Nice try, Sam. I appreciate it but you and I have to go back out on the river tomorrow to check on some decrepit docks and a couple of beached power boats that must have drifted downstream from somewhere in Massachusetts. I've got them secured to boulders and trees for the time being but I don't know if they're stolen yet or just broken away from their moorings. That's gonna' be a whole day shot and then you're on call Thursday and Friday night and I can't have you tied up in the boathouse working on the boats. Damn!"

The Marine Patrol Officers stood by the stair rail at the edge of the upper parking area and said nothing for a few minutes. Sam continued to let Smalls fume. *I'll let him calm down a little and then bring up the Hanks question. It'll be a good way to change the subject.* Smalls was still pacing the edge of the parking lot and once in a while would bend down to pick up a rock and throw it toward the water.

After a few minutes Sam piped up, "Hey Sarge, not to change the subject but did you ever find anything out about those guys in the Checkmate that murdered Hanks?" Smalls turned around and looked Sam square in the eyes, "What brought that up?" Sam looked out at the water again and said, "I drifted past the accident scene Monday and it brought back some memories." Smalls walked back toward Sam, "Look ... those guys are long gone, Sam. Alban pulled me off the case that same summer. Who knows what happened to them." Sam was staring back into Small's eyes and realized Smalls hadn't answered his question. Sam said, "Yeah I know all that but you looked around for weeks ... double patrols. You didn't find anything?" Smalls stared at the ground for a minute as if he was trying to remember. "Well, I checked out some marinas up river. Went as far as I could go before the big dam. Saw some Checkmate class boats but couldn't say for sure if any of them were the one I was looking for. It was dark the night of the accident and descriptors (identifying description of the subject) were absent. Boat's color, bow numbers ... pretty much had nothing to go on." Sam tried to look indifferent with what Smalls was saying. He said nothing when Smalls stopped talking, waited a few seconds then picked up a stone and threw it at the river.

"What's this all about Sam?" Sam glanced back at the sergeant and said, "Just wondering. Nothing ever came of it. Seems liked we just let the whole thing fade away." Smalls smiled and said, "Well that's partly the fault of you and your buddy Jake Farmer. First Farmer gets the whole place riled up with his suspension and then you go after him and get mixed up in a firefight in another state. Things were happening way too fast around here!" Sam just nodded his head as he stared at the ground. Still looking at the ground, Sam asked, "Did you get to talk to any of the marina owners or attendants?" "Well yeah, but you know how that goes ... no one wants to get involved so no one knows anything."

Sam tried to remain matter of fact, "So, you said you saw other Checkmates upriver?" Smalls said, "Oh yeah, as a matter of fact, there was one marina that had more than any of the others. I think they called it Speed Dreamers. Kind of a ritzy place. No one would even look at you, let alone talk about a murder." He paused, "Yeah, now I remember. That was the high class place that called Alban and told him to call me off … that I was offending his customers." A shiver went up Sam's back. O*kay, I've got a place to start. Now to get a look at those incident reports. Better distract Smalls now so he doesn't get suspicious.* He looked skyward and distracted Smalls by suddenly pointing out over the river, "Look at that eagle! That must be the same one I watched attack a black duck the other day. What a beauty!"

Smalls looked up and gave the eagle a cursory glance. Sam tried to act as if the whole conversation was desultory … just matter of fact. Then he shrugged his shoulders and said, "Well, okay Sarge … See you in the morning. I'm going to get some lunch. I'll start on the equipment inventory this afternoon. Tonight I'm on call, so have a good afternoon if I don't see you." Smalls just nodded and said, "Yeah, I might get Sawyer to help me order the parts for tune-ups on both boats.

Takes a day to come in, so maybe I'll see you this afternoon at the boathouse." Sam was already walking toward his truck. Without turning around he just waved a hand in the air as a parting good-bye, got into his pick-up and drove off.

Smalls watched Sam leave the upper parking lot, shook his head and murmured to himself, "Don't see how I'm gonna' fit those boat tune-ups in." Smalls kicked a few more stones and headed off to get into his truck.

The next day Sam and Marine Sergeant Mike Smalls spent most of the day rounding up beached boats between the Thompson Dam and the Massachusetts state line. It was a lot of work since the water was so high and fast this time of year.

Normal anchoring points were either missing or covered by high water and the current's speed made maneuvering difficult. Sam played the part of first mate and did all the line handling while Smalls drove. Smalls was a good skipper and boat handler and Sam felt comfortable because he could concentrate on doing his own job while Smalls did the rest. The two officers worked well together, each anticipating the others moves with hardly a word spoken.

The loose trees, bushes, and parts of boat docks that had been freed from their homes were a constant danger to anyone operating a boat in the river. Part of Sam's job as first mate was to look for those threats and give the skipper a direction to steer the boat in. Finally, Smalls yelled over the wind, "Hey Sam, let's take a break. I'll pull into that little lagoon over there. You can break out the coffee while I grab a smoke." Sam replied without looking back since he had to keep his eyes open for free floating logs, "Okay, Sarge. Sounds good."

Smalls pulled into a little lagoon off the river where the water was flat with no current. "How's she feel," Sam asked. "I noticed you're doing a lot of back and forth with the throttle." Sam was concerned that maybe the tune-ups should have been done even before Alban's requested date. "Ahh, she's been acting like a pig. Lost ignition a couple of times and had to restart her on the fly. That's probably what you heard. Choke seems like it's stuck or something … just not choking right … maybe just bad gas." Sam raised his eyebrows, "Maybe we ought to bring her in now and finish towing these stray boats later." Smalls thought for a moment, "Maybe you're right. I don't feel very confident towing these bad boys across that current. At least I've got their hull numbers and registrations (boat's registration paperwork). Sam felt relieved, "Yeah, I agree. This is a nice secluded spot with no current and I can secure them to those tree trunks

over there. Should be fine until we can get back out here."
It was agreed to leave the boats in the lagoon until they got
the Carolina working better so Smalls and Sam secured the
boats, finished their coffees and headed for the boat ramp.

As Smalls pulled up to their new boat dock, Sam threw a
line to lasso the first pier. It caught hold, and Smalls, seeing
this, shifted the engine to NEUTRAL. Sam pulled the
line taut to bring the Carolina's bow in close to the dock.
As Smalls began shutting down the boat's electronics, Sam
looked back across the river to where they had left the boats.
"Don't worry, Sarge, I have them secured pretty well … and
they're out of view of the general public. They're not going
anywhere." Smalls nodded in agreement, "We'll get 'em
in the morning. This will give me time to do paperwork
on them, and call the owners." Sam stared at Smalls. *We
shouldn't have even been out there today if that engine was running
so badly. Hope he gets Sawyer on it tonight.*

The two men went their different ways. Smalls headed
for the P.D. where he could do the paperwork and phone
calling from his office. Sam went back to the boathouse
and finished up the day doing equipment inventories on the
Avon and the Carolina. The Avon, being of the inflatable
type was pretty straightforward and didn't require too much
effort. It was a work boat and the equipment she carried was
out in the open and generally hung from rope life lines that
were attached at the top of the gunnels, around the boat's
perimeter.

Sam looked at the clock on the wall. *Five o'clock. Done for
the day. Haven't seen Corporal Sawyer come in … or maybe I
just missed him one of those times I had my head buried in the
Carolina's hold. I'll just check the boathouse log to see if anyone
showed up.* Sam walked over to the Sign In log that hung
on the wall near the boathouse entrance. Anyone coming

in to work a shift in the boathouse was supposed to sign in here. The space was blank so Sam called Dispatch on the boathouse phone. Evidently Marine Corporal Sawyer had called out this afternoon. Sam thought for a moment. *Hmm, Smalls is working out of his office this afternoon so he must know Sawyer called out. I guess he's going to do the tune ups himself. I'm outta' here.* He walked out the door and made sure the outer door to the boathouse was locked, and headed for home.

★ ★ ★ ★

CHAPTER 4

Thursday morning was just another day. Sam knew he was off for the day and on call beginning at six PM. Peg had left for work already and the boys were at school. He walked out to the kitchen and poured himself a cup of hot, black coffee. Sam sipped the coffee and walked over to the kitchen door and out onto the farmer's porch that surrounded his cabin. It was a bright, sunny day with clear skies. A little morning wind with some seasonal chill in the air but otherwise a typical April morning.

Sam looked up into the sky. No honkers yet. They should be returning from the south soon. He took another sip of his coffee and wondered. *What will tonight bring. Been quiet on the river so far. This is about the time people who can't wait for the regular boating season to venture out onto the river … ready or not. Water is still way to high and fast for safe boating. I hope the day shift keeps an eye on the boat ramp and whoever may be trying to launch. Usually people cut corners this time of year just to get out there.* Sam shook his head in a sidewise fashion. *Aah, I can't be watching all the time. Better get some breakfast and get my day started.* With that, Sam began his daily chores around the cabin and busied himself with washing his truck.

The hours seemed to pass fairly quickly. Soon it was four thirty in the afternoon. Peg came home from work and Sam was under his truck changing the oil. He heard her pull into the driveway and watched her feet as they came up alongside his truck. He screwed the oil drain plug back into the oil pan was staring at the feet and ankles that had come to a halt where his own feet protruded from underneath the truck. "Hello," Peg didn't bother to bend to look under the truck. "I brought home hamburgers for you to grill before you go on call. Can you start them about five thirty?" Sam smiled, "Sure. I'm done here for now. Let me get washed up and I'll get right on it." Peg just nodded her head as if Sam could see her and went in the house with the groceries.

After dinner Sam did the dishes and helped the boys with their homework. He glanced at his watch. It was 7 PM and no calls. *So far, so good*, he thought. He got up from the kitchen table and looked out one of the windows facing west. *What a pretty sunset!* The sun was starting to drop behind the west hills casting an orange glow over the darkening ridge. The sky was still cloudless which enhanced the sunset's radiance.

The night continued with no disturbances. The boys had gone to bed and Peg came in to the living room, "I'm kind of tired. I'm going to bed too." Sam said goodnight and gave her a peck on the cheek." Peg stopped and turned back toward Sam, "Wake me if you have to go out on a call … Okay?" Sam looked up from the fireplace and said, "Only if it's not too late." Peg smirked back at him, turned and went to bed.

Suddenly, the phone rang. It was Thompson Police Dispatch. Sam picked up the phone, "Moody, here." "Sam, get the boat. You have a small family in the water below the Thompson falls. They went out for a sunset cruise, got too close to the dam, and went over. Witnesses say everyone seems okay for now but they've been in the water for ten minutes … Two adults and two children. They're in the water and holding onto the sides of the boat. We're worried about hypothermia. Access through the lower boat launch. EXPEDITE!"

Sam was already in his Class C uniform. A simple uniform which was comprised of a button down uniform shirt and blue jeans. He ran to the kitchen door and threw on his issue lined windbreaker and Class B baseball cap. Sam was through the door and in his truck in no time. He sped out of his gravel driveway and threw on his red light as soon as he hit the main road. "419 responding and enroute to the boathouse. Code one." (law enforcement code that means lights and sirens. No stopping for traffic lights or other hindrances.) Dispatch came back, "Roger 419." There was a pause then Dispatch continued, "419, standby for accident details." Dispatch came back, "419, subject boat is a low gunnel Bass Tracker, aluminum V-hull type, color red. Boat is overturned, hull facing the sky. Held in place by an anchor thrown out before they went over the falls. Victims are holding onto the boat as long as the anchor holds. Water exposure time now at fifteen minutes."

Sam was now speeding down the main road that led to the boathouse where the Carolina was being stored for repairs. It would be ten minutes at best before Sam arrived. He glanced down at his speedometer. In the dark cab the green dash board numbers lit up and mixed with the red strobe light mounted on his dashboard. Fifty miles an hour, sixty, seventy miles an hour. *Probably hold her here*, Sam thought. *Got a tight turn coming up.* Sam could now see the turn he'd need to take to get to the boathouse and a thought crossed his mind. *Hope Smalls got a chance to tune the Carolina up. Water looked a little faster when I drove by the river this morning.* Then he dismissed the thought. *Can't worry about that now just got to get those people out of the water.*

As usual, police cruisers diverted traffic from the street that led to the boathouse and blocked the oncoming lanes in front of the boathouse gate. Sam had now slowed to fifty miles an hour and again down to forty as he made the turn into the gate. It felt as if the truck made that turn on two tires with the passenger side of the truck airborne. He reached up and switched off the flashing red light, pulled up next to the boathouse and hit the ground running as he dashed for the boathouse entrance.

The usual obstacle course was still there so he found himself ducking snowplows that hung from the ceiling, jumping over lawn tractors and tripping on various lawn implements that lay askew on the garage floor. It was a dangerous sprint, especially in the dark.

Finally, Sam got to the boat's garage. He flew through the door to see the Carolina quietly awaiting him. She sat in the boat bay ready to go, awaiting her next mission. Sam flipped the garage door opener switch and the bay doors started to open. Now more sirens could be heard and then he saw two flashing red lights come through the gate entrance … one behind the other. Sam's radio crackled, "408 and 410 arrival – boathouse." By their radio numbers Sam knew it was Smalls and Marine Corporal Sawyer. Smalls ran up to the bay door and started to help Sam ready the Carolina's hitch to accept the tow vehicle's tongue while Corporal Sawyer backed Smalls' truck toward the waiting Carolina.

"Sam, Sawyer and I got this. We'll tow the Carolina to the lower boat launch and meet you down there. Make sure the ramp is clear so we can dump the boat right away. Sawyer and I are in the boat. You head up stream after we launch and direct us from the ledge below Bridge Lane."

Sam's heart sank. *Once again, I'm the first arrival and everybody else gets to do the glory stuff.* Trying not to show how he really felt, Sam looked Smalls in the eyes and told the Marine Sergeant he'd have the ramp ready for immediate launch. Sam left the garage and jogged to his own truck for the ride to the lower boat launch.

★ ★ ★ ★

CHAPTER 5

The lower boat launch was dark and quiet. The sun had set and there was no moon. Anyone that had been out in the river would have come in at least an hour ago. Sam looked over the boat ramp. Nothing in the way. Then he heard Smalls on the radio. "408 to Headquarters." "Go ahead 408." Smalls came back, "I am approaching the lower boat launch entrance. ETA is two minutes. Will be immediate launch." Dispatch intervened with, "408, be advised parties have been in the water twenty-five minutes. Approaching hypothermic threat." Smalls replied, "408 roger. Backing Marine One in now."

Smalls climbed into the boat and got behind the helm, opened the radio box, and began turning on the Carolina's electronics. Sawyer rushed about the deck readying lines and equipment. Sam stayed on the ramp ready to push the Carolina off the trailer. Once in the water, the current would try to grab the boat and pull it downstream so Smalls had to get the prop going as soon as it hit the water. The work on the boat ramp was suddenly interrupted by another vehicle's arrival. It was Captain Fletcher. Fletcher got out of his truck and approached the Carolina. "Smalls! Get that boat in the water … NOW! Those people only have a few minutes left."

Smalls glanced at the captain and replied, "Ready to go, sir." Then nodded to Sam, "Okay, Sam let her slide." Sam held the bowline and pushed the Carolina off her skids. Once the boat hit the water Sam threw the bowline to Sawyer. The prop hit the water and Smalls turned the ignition switch and choked the engine. The Carolina's forty horse engine came to life and Smalls could feel the current trying to pull the Carolina stern first into the dark, cold river. Gently he pushed the throttle to one third reverse power to overcome the current, turned the helm over so the bow was headed up stream and pushed the throttle ahead to one half full throttle FORWARD. The Carolina obeyed and backed out into the river as requested and made a gentle transition to forward way as Smalls increased engine RPM.

It was a clean launch. Sam saluted the Captain as he ran by him in the parking lot. "Where are you going Moody?" Sam turned to look back at the Captain as he ran, "Gotta' get upriver so I can light up the cliff area for Smalls. They're going to be operating pretty close to the cliffs." Sam ran out of the parking lot and onto the train tracks that ran parallel to the river. He pulled out his radio as he ran, "419 – Headquarters. Officer on the gauge." It was a strict rule that once an officer was on the train tracks or gauge, Dispatch be notified immediately. Only in this way could the officer's safety be guaranteed and approaching trains be held up or detoured from an area. "Roger 419," came the reply. "Shutting down the tracks now."

It was dark below Bridge Lane. The water didn't even feel cold any more. The accident victim's bodies were numb and they could feel whatever strength they still had slowly waning. None of the four people in the water could close their hands any longer so they put their arms through a loop of rope the father had desperately rigged from one side of the capsized boat to the other. The line was draped over the upturned hull and allowed them to get their arms in it without having to hold it with their fingers. The life jackets they wore helped keep them afloat but if not for the line draped across the hull, the jackets would have helped the current to carry them away. It was just a helpless situation. Joe Smyth could only watch as his family shivered in the cold water. His two children, eight year old Cindy, and ten year old son Paul, had stopped talking and crying. They just held onto their dad's overturned boat. Jenny, his wife tried to keep the kids talking but now they just stared when she spoke to them. The situation seemed hopeless.

"Is anyone coming," a desperate mother screamed into the air. "Why isn't anyone coming? Where are they?" The question was not really aimed at anyone in particular. Just a frantic mother crying out into the darkness for some kind of hope. "Help … can anyone hear us?" The shouts and screams were futile since the roar of the fast moving rapids drowned out any sound from ten feet away. Joe watched his wife struggle and knew she was way past panic. He was watching his family die a slow death. They didn't deserve this. The pain, the discomfort … the terror. How could he have been so reckless, so irresponsible? He asked himself why he had stayed out in the river past sunset. Now he was paying for that beautiful sunset with his family's lives.

He reached out and grabbed Jenny's arm, "Honey, save your strength. You're using up energy. You need that to keep hold of the kids." She violently jerked her hand away from Joe. "Leave me alone! I'm doing what I need to do." Jenny was half crying and half screaming. Joe kept his eye on the anchor line that still held his boat from going down river. He had managed to throw the anchor in a last ditch effort when he saw how close to the falls he was. The anchor caught above the dam and the anchor line payed out as the boat went over. Now it was the only thing that held them in place where rescuers could get to them. If that anchor let go or the line broke they would all be doomed.

Cindy began to close her eyes. Hypothermia was beginning to set in and she was starting to fall asleep. Jenny yelled, "Cindy! Don't go to sleep. Keep your eyes open. Look at Mommy!" Jenny grabbed the little girl's arm and kept shaking it. "Cindy!" Cindy's eyes were closed. Jenny let go the safety line and reached for Cindy in an attempt to shake or slap the little girl back into a conscious state. The rushing water got hold of Jenny's body and broke it free from the boat. Joe had anticipated the problem and reached out in time to grab his wife by the life jacket. He still had hold of the life line with his left hand and struggled to get Jenny back to the boat with his right. Finally, with a supreme effort, Joe got Jenny back to where she could once again, hold the lifeline. "Ju..ju..st hold on Hon..ey. Som..Some.. one must..must have se..seen us. Were … other boats … out here. Pro..bly called it in …"

Back on the train tracks Sam could hear Smalls' radio transmissions. "408 to Dispatch. Water extremely rough. Loose tree trunks from upstream causing collision threat. Can't see the capsized boat or survivors yet." "Roger 408. Hypothermic threat now at thirty-five minutes." "Roger that. 408 out." Sam broke into a full sprint. He glanced down at the river to his left and fifty feet below. He was abreast of the Carolina. He could see her running lights and Sawyer's searchlight. Her headway was slow but Smalls had to keep changing course to avoid being torpedoed by the huge logs coming downstream.

Sam got to a point on the cliffs abreast of the accident scene ahead of the Carolina. The cliff went straight down to the water where huge boulders lay scattered at its base. It was a frightening scene. Just ahead of the boulders and about fifty feet offshore was the boat with four people clinging to it. Sam got as close as he could to the cliff's edge and hung onto a tree that hung out over the water. When he got a good purchase on the tree and cliff's edge, he aimed his spotlight down onto the stricken boat. The boat and people were now a white spot on the dark river's surface.

Jenny noticed the light and looked up toward Sam's position. "Joe, some ... some..body sees us." She was beginning to slur her words. Joe didn't reply. He was almost spent and had all he could do just to hold onto the life line and Paul's lifejacket. The children were quiet and not moving.

Sam keyed his radio, "408 from 419. I have the boat and victims in my spotlight. Look for the light about fifty feet off the cliff's edge, 100 feet ahead of you." There was a pause, and then a second search light illuminated the grim scene below the cliffs. "Got 'em, 419. Heading for them now." Joe had just run out of strength and lost his grip on the life line. The current took Joe from the safety of the boat and dragged him away from his family instantly. Sam keyed his radio, "408 you've got one coming your way. Lost his grip. Try to retrieve him on your starboard side." Sawyer's searchlight tracked the approaching floater and Smalls tried to angle the Carolina so the floater would come right to the Carolina's side. At the last moment Smalls turned the helm over and throttled back to IDLE slowing the forward momentum of the boat. The current carried Joe right up to the Carolina and his body slammed right into the boat's starboard side. Sawyer was ready and dragged Joe over the gunnel. Joe looked up and could barely speak, "G..G.. Get my f..f..fam. P..P..Pe..lllee..ase." Then Joe's head fell back onto the Carolina's deck.

Sawyer checked the victim over. "Sarge, he's full stage hypothermic and may be having a heart attack. Barely a pulse, eyes rolled back, breathing is faint." Smalls kept his eyes on the river and was preparing to throttle up and get the Carolina back on course to the rest of the victims. He yelled to Sawyer above the roar of the angry river, "Roll him over on his side … he may have swallowed some water, then tilt his head back and open his airway before you start anything else."

Suddenly the whole boat was violently pushed sideways, starboard to port, as if another boat had crashed into them. A large log had just found the Carolina and rammed her starboard side, knocking Sawyer off Joe and into the right knee of Smalls. Smalls fell to the floor wincing in pain and the Carolina spun out of control turning circles in the current as she drifted down river. Smalls collected himself on the deck in front of the helm and dragged himself to a standing position again. His right knee felt like a hot poker had just pierced it from side to side. The injured skipper managed to get back to the helm and busied himself with getting the Carolina back under control. "Sawyer get back to work on this guy." Then he picked up the mic, "408 to 419."

Sam was still hanging over the river showing his spotlight on the distressed victims. He brought his radio to his mouth, "419 here. Parties are losing it, 408. They have about five minutes left." Smalls came back, "Okay, I'm on my way. Picked up the floater and Sawyer is working on him. I'm coming in fast. You're my eyes now. Keep that spot light right on the center of the scene." "Roger that, 408. I've got your lights now. Come starboard a little. You're about 100 feet downstream of them."

Dispatch listened helplessly to the radio transmissions between Smalls and Moody. Without being able to see the situation for what it was the transmissions painted a picture of terror and near defeat. Dispatcher Jordan Marsh D30, had one hand on his earphones and the other on his computer keyboard. *These guys are too busy to think of the next step. I have to request ambulances now.* Jordan reached up and depressed the EMR (Emergency Medical Response) button on the console in front of him. The button illuminated at Jordan's prompting. "Thompson Dispatch requesting two ambulances … one for cardiac support, one for severe hypothermia. Destination is Thompson lower boat launch, Connecticut River – Parsons Road section. All victims hypothermic. Other injuries unknown at this time." EMR acknowledged and two ambulances were speeding to the scene.

Smalls approached the capsized boat and its victims and Sawyer had Joe Smyth stabilized and breathing for the time being. He had stripped off all of the man's clothes and covered him with three wool blankets. Sawyer ran to the Carolina's bow and prepared to take on victims. Smalls skillfully brought the Carolina up alongside the capsized boat. He had to keep the throttle open to one half full FORWARD just to hold the Carolina in place while Sawyer positioned himself over the Carolina's starboard side to retrieve the cold, soaked people. Sawyer grabbed Cindy from her mother and placed her in a prone position on the Carolina's foredeck in front of the helm, then went back for Paul. Sawyer had to literally drag the ten year old up and over the side. The Carolina's freeboard was about eighteen inches. It was a chore for any man considering the water soaked clothing and bulky life jacket. He placed Paul on the deck next to Cindy and went back for the mother, Jenny. Jenny looked up into Sawyers eyes like he was a kind of welcome angel. She tried to mouth something although talking was now out of the question. It may have been thank you or thank god but the look was just that of extreme relief.

As Sawyer wrestled Jenny's limp body into the boat Smalls yelled over the windscreen, "Cover 'em … and get down on the deck with them. I'm making a port turn into the current at full throttle." Sawyer positioned his body so he almost completely covered the mother and two children to share some of his body heat as Smalls wrestled the Carolina around in a one hundred eighty degree turn down river. Smalls picked up the mic and keyed it, "408 to headquarters. We are enroute to the ramp with all parties. Have ambulances meet us on approach. Parties are semi-conscious and will not be able to walk." Dispatch acknowledged Smalls and told him the ambulances were already there and awaiting his arrival.

Smalls could see the lower boat ramp as it was illuminated by some of the police cruisers attending the scene. He keyed his mic again, "419 from 408. Get down to the ramp ASAP. Getting ready to transfer parties to EMR. I'm injured and going with them but we still have to get that boat out of the river. Do you copy?" Sam was already out of the tree and running as fast as his legs allowed. Out of breath, Sam managed to roger Smalls as he made for the lower boat ramp.

Sam had changed places with Smalls in the Carolina. Smalls' knee was so badly injured the ambulance took him along with the cardiac patient. Fletcher stood and watched the two boat skippers as they traded places. "Sam look out for logs … they're coming down fast." Sam just nodded back as the Carolina slid back down into the dark river.

As Sam got the Carolina pointed upstream he yelled to Sawyer in the bow, "Get to the bow and hold on. I'm gonna' open her up." Sam was now the ranking officer in the boat. He was the boat's skipper which gave him authority over any rank that might be aboard. "Keep that searchlight forward and watch for logs."

Sam slowly moved the throttle ahead until he was at least three quarters full FORWARD. This allowed the Carolina to get up on plane (boat riding at near water surface and flat) with more control over the rushing black current. Suddenly Sawyer shouted, "Sam, go to port!" Sam swung the helm over and watched as a telephone pole sized log slid down the starboard side of the boat. "Starboard – starboard," Sawyer was yelling over the river's thrumming noise. Another near miss down the Carolina's port side. The obstacle course continued until Sawyer raised his right hand for Sam's attention. Then he brought his whole arm down to horizontal pointing to a position about thirty degrees off the starboard bow. Sam angled the Carolina over to the capsized craft. As he neared the wreck he noticed she was held fast by a line that came out of the water by her bow and again disappeared into the black water above the dam.

"Sawyer, I'm going to pull up along the port side and hold us there while you tie on to the skeg. Signal when you're tied on and I'll move us forward to the bow. When you're ready, cut the anchor line." Sam knew that as soon as he cut the line the strain that was on the anchor line would then be owned by the Carolina. Sawyer nodded and began attempting to attach a tow line to the capsized boat skeg. He made several attempts while Sam tried to keep the Carolina steady in the current. Their position in the current made them extremely vulnerable to approaching logs and debris.

Just as Sawyer made his fourth attempt to lasso the skeg, the Carolina broke from her position at the stern of the stricken boat and started drifting violently backward. First a jerk, then uncontrolled speed and direction. Sam had nothing from the throttle or the helm. The Carolina was moving backward and picking up speed by the second. The rushing current began to push her toward the glacial boulders that lay scattered at the bottom of the Bridge Lane cliffs. The engine had stalled. There was no power and no steerage. "Sam … Sam! Get her going. We're gonna' hit those rocks," a panicked Marine Corporal Sawyer started to run toward the helm. "Stay in the bow, John," Sam said as he fiddled with the choke and ignition. Sawyer watched as the back of the Carolina's Bimini canvas top brushed against overhanging tree limbs that extended out from the trees on shore. "Sam … we're gonna' hit!" Sam never looked up but kept his concentration on getting the engine started again. The Carolina seemed doomed. Her starboard transom was three feet from the first boulder when the engine caught. Sam felt it catch and shoved the throttle to full FORWARD. A rooster tail of water shot into the air as the Carolina lurched forward. Sam held on tight to the helm. It was like a roller coaster ride. Sawyer fell onto the deck back toward the helm due to the sudden change in direction. The Carolina was under power and on her way again.

Sam pulled away from the rocks and boulders that had almost claimed his boat. *Damn Smalls never tuned the son of a bitch. She's running choppier than ever now. Can't risk the crew or the boat under these circumstances … especially for a wrecked boat.* When Sawyer got to his feet Sam said, "I'm going to approach the wreck one more time. Get an anchor buoy with short line ready. We'll drop it by the boat as we pass so it can be seen as an obstruction. You've only got one chance to make a good toss."

The Carolina approached the wreck and then angled away so her starboard side faced the wreck's stern. "Now!" Sam yelled. Sawyer made a good throw and the buoy's anchor went under. Sam throttled up and steered for the center of the river. "Watch for the buoy, John." Sawyer scanned the wreck with his spotlight as the Carolina departed the scene. Suddenly the orange marker buoy popped up alongside the overturned wreck and held its position in the current.

"Marker's good, Sam." "Okay," replied Sam, without looking back. "Have a seat. We're going home." It was then that Sam remembered his promise to Peg. *Damn it! I forgot to tell Peg I had an emergency.*

★ ★ ★ ★

CHAPTER 6

The next morning came all too soon. Sam found himself sitting in the roll call room with the rest of the department. He and his two buddies, Stafford and James sat in their usual spot in one of the rear corners of the room. The room was buzzing about last night's rescue. Smalls and Corporal Sawyer sat together in the front row silently. Pat James turned toward Sam, "What went on out there last night? Sounded like you guys had your hands full." Sam just nodded his head and allowed a smirk but said nothing. Tom Stafford interrupted and offered in a low tone. "I'm sure we're about to find out, Pat. Leave him alone."

Lieutenant Alban entered the room and everyone stood up. Alban nodded without looking up and said, "Okay, okay … sit." Alban shuffled through some meeting notes and began calling roll. Alban left the rescue for the last order of business. "Gentlemen, last night we had a rescue below the dam near the cliffs at Bridge Lane." It was then that he looked up. He looked Marine Sergeant Smalls in the eyes and panned over to Sawyer. "Seems as if things could have gone better. The victims were in the water for almost forty-five minutes before we got them into the Carolina. The father and little girl are still critical. All of them were well into severe hypothermia and the father had a mild heart attack." Alban stopped reading from his keynotes and looked up. He paused and looked about the room. "This is unacceptable gentlemen! An entire family almost bought it last night." There was another pause then a repeat of the latter but louder, "An entire family! I hope that wasn't your best effort." Alban shuffled his papers on the podium and without looking at the group of officers said, "Smalls, Sawyer, Moody … in my office … five minutes. Dismissed!"

The room became deadly quiet. Everyone stood as Alban left the room. There were muffled conversations about what was probably going to happen. Smalls and Sawyer left together without saying a word. Smalls was on crutches so Sawyer led, holding the door for him. Sam started from the back of the room to catch up with Smalls as everyone turned to watch him exit. No one said a word except Tom Stafford. "Hey Sam." Sam stopped and turned around. Tom Continued, "It's gonna' be fine. You did your job." Sam showed no emotion, turned and walked out of the room.

The three marine officers took their positions in front of Alban's desk. Smalls was seated because of his knee injury and his crutches leaned against a filing cabinet. He sat bolt upright and at attention. Sawyer and Moody stood, also at attention, next to Smalls.

Lieutenant Alban sat quietly behind his desk, still fuming and glared at the three nervous officers standing before him. He was a big man with short, sandy colored hair slowly giving way to grey. He stood at six foot one inch tall and weighed in at 260 pounds. His broad shoulders and intimidating scowl made him a hard person to question and it was understood he didn't tolerate excuses or lying.

Finally, Alban stood from his desk and addressed the men. "What in hell were you guys doing last night? Did you think that because I was out of town you could dog it a little? Did you think I wouldn't get a report? I got a report all right. Fletcher reported the whole thing. A lousy report like that had to be filed by our own Captain. It's now been circulated to town and state offices. We look like shit!"

No one spoke a word. Alban started pacing back and forth in front of the men. He stopped in front of Sam, "You know …, Alban paused for effect, "Mister Moody, you seem to have been in here quite a bit lately. Why is that?" Sam just continued to look forward. Alban just glared at Sam for a few seconds longer then moved on to Smalls. "Marine Sergeant Smalls … you do realize that the response time in getting Marine One into the water was wayyyy unacceptable?" Smalls continued to look forward, "We did our best LT …," Alban cut him off, "Your best? Your best almost caused the lives of four citizens!" He paused then started again, "Two people may not make it and one 'ems a kid! Your best!?" Smalls began again, "Sir, the water was high and fast and the logs coming from upriver were all over the place. One of 'em hit the Carolina amidships, starboard side. That's how I wrecked my knee. Besides, … you gave me until Saturday to get the boats ready." "Enough," Alban was glaring at all three officers. "I know what the conditions were. I read the report … and I do not want to hear excuses. So you hurt your knee. That's too bad. Poor, Mikey. Your jobs are to serve and protect … no matter what the cost. If those loose tree trunks are starting to scare you Sergeant maybe you ought to think about a different line of work."

Alban was pacing the room again and kept the men at attention. He went to the window behind his desk and stood staring out of it with his back to the men. After a time he said, "Do you men know what the consequences are here?" Alban was still staring out the window. "I mean outside of the victim's outcomes or your jobs?" Still, no one spoke. The Fire Department wants to take over river rescue and recovery." Alban turned to look at his officers again. "A show like this makes us look like the high school rowing team could have done better. How am I supposed to explain that no one could have done better?" Alban paused a moment, then continued. "How can I say it was most definitely us that should have been out there and not them?" The three marine officers remained at attention and said nothing.

Alban looked at Sam. "Moody! You couldn't even recover a wrecked boat! You cut the anchor line because it was getting too rough out there?" Moody came back quick, "Called it like I saw it LT …," Alban cut him off, "Stow it Mister. I don't want to hear it." Sam ignored Alban's demand to stand down and was determined to say his piece. "I was the skipper sir. My choice was based on the conditions. I wasn't going to risk boat and crew over an already wrecked boat to save face regardless of who was watching."

Alban's face was now beat red. "Moody, one more word and you are suspended." He turned his attention back to Smalls. "Sergeant. I thought I gave you distinct orders to tune those boats last week. Moody here was supposed to relay that message … or maybe he didn't find time to do that." Alban glared back at Sam. Smalls spoke up, "Moody gave me the message sir and we divvied up the work assignments. I had paperwork to do on the boats that drifted down from Massachusetts and Corporal Sawyer tuned the Carolina and the Avon." John Sawyer's face now reddened up. Alban looked at Sawyer, "Why did the engine stall on Moody if they were so well tuned up, Corporal?" Sawyer still looking straight ahead said, "I didn't tune either of the boats, LT." Smalls broke from attention and turned his head toward

Sawyer, "I left you specific instructions on the work board in the boathouse, Corporal. Wednesday afternoon." Sawyer's voice was now shaking, "Went home early on Wednesday, Sarge. Never saw it." Now it all made sense to Sam. That's why he didn't see Sawyer show up and scratch his name off the work board. Smalls would never have known Sawyer didn't get the message.

Alban recognized the snafu in communications. This was his marine division … all good officers. He also recognized last night's performance was not typical of them. Alban strode over to the window again and looked out. Without looking at the men he said, "Think about everything you guys did last night and how you can do it better. Dismissed." The three officers turned and exited Alban's office.

Smalls headed for his office where he could be alone. Sawyer and Moody knew not to approach him in this kind of mood, so they just let him go. Instead, the two officers walked down the hallway in silence. Eventually they came to the cafeteria where they stopped. Sawyer looked at Sam, "What are we supposed to do now?" "Well, I'd get to tuning those boats before anyone brings it up again … and do the best job you have ever done, John. I'm going to go over to the records department to look up some things." The two officers bid each other farewell as they went their own ways.

Sam began to research the two year old file about rookie Steve Hanks and his murder on the river. He found a quiet spot in the back of the room and began poring over the files. He read the report Alban had given of what he had witnessed before he lost consciousness that night and also the reports of all the other officers that had been on scene. Sam pulled Smalls' incident reports and put them aside for the time being. He remembered Smalls was stationed down river of the rafted up Checkmate and Carolina and approached the accident scene from behind as the accident unfolded.

The Avon's skipper description of the scene was exactly as Sam remembered it but Smalls noted in the account that the night was moonless and from his position couldn't see the Checkmate's hull numbers. Color descriptors were that it appeared in the darkness as a 'mostly white boat with a wide stripe below the gunnel.' The stripe could have been any of the darker colors but with the light shed by the Carolina's searchlights, appeared red. There wasn't much else about the lowrider to talk about except her passengers and driver.

Of course the driver who had spoken directly to Alban as he attempted to board the boat had been described as a white Caucasian, 25 to 28 years old, medium build, about six feet tall, short dark hair, with a mustache and goatee. Some descriptors were missing because his two passengers had been positioned in front of him as he spoke to the lieutenant. The other boaters were also Caucasian, around mid–twenties, but seemed slighter in build about one hundred sixty pounds, one with short, dark hair and the other with dark, shoulder length. Neither man had any facial hair. Their dress was casual jeans and pocket tee shirts. One of the two men that shielded the driver from Alban also wore a baseball type hat, which was turned backward.

Sam searched the report for any kind of detail. *Come on Alban … what was on the hats … anything?* Sam continued to read the report. *Ahh, here's something.* Alban's testimony reflected the fact that the hat worn by the driver had lettering on it, white or gold, that advertised, … 's Speed Tr', or something to that effect. The entire logo had not been discernable. There were two willow trees-one on either end of the phrase as it arched across the front of the hat.

Below the arched title on the hat was another phrase which wasn't recognizable. The other man's hat that was worn backwards and had an emblem on the back that depicted the figure of a beautiful woman holding onto a long pole but leaning away from it, and more arched lettering under the emblem that said, 'At The Swamp.' *Well that's a different kind of name. I'm going to find out where that place is. Maybe he's a local there.*

The door to records opened and Lieutenant Alban walked in. Sam looked back down and at the computer, as if he hadn't noticed him. He started closing down the computer system and shoved the notes he had taken into one of the pockets of his BDU cargo pants. Alban glanced over and saw Sam, thought nothing of it, and continued with his own quest. Sam waited for Alban to disappear and hurried over to the copy machine to make duplicates of his new found information. *I've got to speak to Alban about all this but this is not the time.* He collected his copies and left for the day. The weekend was here and it would give him time to go over his new found information.

★ ★ ★ ★

CHAPTER 7

After dinner, Sam went to his office in the loft above the garage. He needed to go somewhere quiet where he could study more about the research done on the Hanks' accident. Just as he settled into his desk chair Peg called him from the exterior staircase that led to his lair. "Sam, its Friday night. Can't you put that stuff away for a little while? The boys want to go to the movies." Sam got up from the desk and went to the loft's outside entrance that led to the staircase, "I'll be down in about a half hour, Honey. Can you get them ready to go? We still have plenty of time to get to the movies." Peg looked up the wooden stairway at Sam, "I still haven't forgotten that you left for that rescue last night without telling me." Sam smiled down at her and said, "Well, I'm still here to say I forgot and that I'm sorry." Peg turned to walk away and said, "Wise ass! See how far that gets you next time."

Sam sat back down at his desk and started pouring over the incident reports on Hanks' accident. He began to envision the whole scene again; how Alban approached the lowrider as it sat dark and still in the black water. He thought about the lieutenant's warning to the crew to stay alert and remembered his hail to the anchored vessel of who we were and to prepare to raft up. Even as a rookie,

Sam had realized something was wrong. The lowrider's occupants remained quiet until hailed again as the Carolina got closer. Sam remembered looking at the Checkmate class boat and how he watched the three men that stood behind the Checkmate's windshield as Alban spoke to them. It seemed strange that the passengers stood in front of the driver who had ultimate responsibility for the craft. The driver's face was chiseled and adorned with well attended facial hair. 'This isn't my boat,' the driver had told Alban. Sam sat back in his chair and thought for a moment. *We never did get to see any paperwork saying whose boat it really was.* Sam concentrated harder. *I remember the hat he wore and on one of the other passengers. Never saw the logos though. What were three guys in their mid-twenties doing out in an expensive boat like that … and one that wasn't theirs?*

"Sam! The kids are waiting." Peg was again at the bottom of his loft stairs. "Okay, coming," Sam said as he rose from his desk. *I have to run through this with Stafford and James tomorrow. We'll see what they remember.*

★ ★ ★ ★

Because the three wardens had been rookies at the time, literally on their first cruise, and the Hanks case came up while they were at the academy, they had not been required to appear in court. Signed statements as to what they saw were all that was required. Now, they had to depend on what Sam could uncover and the testimonies of Alban and Smalls.

Tom Stafford and Pat James met Sam at one of their favorite coffee houses near the edge of town. They picked a table in a far corner of the room where they could talk without being overheard. Sam reiterated his findings so far and showed them the notes he had pulled from the Records Department incident reports. Stafford was first to speak, "Have you talked to Alban about this?" Sam took a sip from his coffee, "Not yet. He's still pretty hot over the rescue Thursday night. I will though. Timing isn't right." James spoke up, "What in hell is he pissed at you for? You weren't even in the boat when they pulled the victims out of the water. Then you got in the boat at Fletcher's request to rescue an already sunken vessel … under dangerous conditions." Sam looked at both of his buddies and smiled. "I don't think it was actually us he was made at. He mentioned response times and how the Fire Department wants to take over river rescue and recoveries. I think he was more upset at the situation and what it could mean if the wrong administrators wanted to push the idea." Both Stafford and James just shook their heads. James finally piped up, "Their job is to put out fires and save homes and buildings. Leave the river stuff to us."

Sam brought the conversation back to the matter at hand. Both Stafford and James added to what they remembered about the Hanks accident and everyone seemed in compliance with one another. Suddenly, James had a revelation, "Hey, now I remember something about that Checkmate. I dove into the water to get Hanks, and that Checkmate guy almost ran me over. I got a glimpse of some wording on the stern as it went past." James was speaking slower as he thought about what he was remembering, "Saw the word Stre … Streak … Streaker, yeah Streaker, that's it … on the starboard side of the stern. Yeah, yeah … it's all coming' back now. It was a Massachusetts reg (boat registration) too. Saw the letters MS on the starboard bow." It was marine law that all Massachusetts registered boats be numbered and displayed on both sides of the vessel's bow.

Sam was incredulous, "You're just remembering that now? After all the hype that went on." James looked disappointed.

"Sam – remember. I had just dove into the water to save an injured comrade. Things were happening so fast … so much information in front of us that was passing by us in mille-seconds. Not to mention the mental aspect of prioritizing the needs at hand which seemed to change just as quickly." Sam nodded his head in agreement, "Sorry, Pat. You're right." Then James added, "Remember, I had a hold of Hanks who was dying in my arms, then Smalls almost ran over both of us as he came up from behind to assist. The only reason he missed us is because you yelled 'Starboard-Starboard.' He pulled the helm over just in time to miss us and ended up crashing into the Carolina." James paused for a moment as if he was envisioning the whole scenario in his mind's eye. Then he continued in a softer tone, "I guess my thoughts were so filled with getting Hanks to safety some of that stuff just went to the back of my memory." Stafford added, "Don't forget – we were whisked off to the academy a week later and because of our newness were only required to give a written statement of what we thought happened." Then he looked back at James, "That is great information, Pat. Good job." James just smiled back but it was obvious he felt a little offended with Sam's remark. It was obvious, as with any accident scene, the people involved see the situation only as it appears to them and how it affects them personally. But now Sam had new information to add to his own investigation.

Sam drained his coffee cup and stood up from the table. "Gotta' go guys … on call again tonight. This was a good talk but we need to do this again and brainstorm more information out of each other. I think we all saw more than we think we did. Pat is proof of that." With that, Sam grabbed his light jacket from the chair and headed for the door. Tom and Pat watched Sam leave and ordered another round of coffees.

★ ★ ★ ★

CHAPTER 8

Sam spent the rest of the evening back up in his loft above the barn's garage area. There were no calls all night and Sam used that time to read over more of the Hanks investigation. Peg had come up to the loft a couple of times to bring him a snack, and the boys, Matt, Steven, and Joey, all took their turns visiting their father in his office above the barn. It was getting late so Sam decided to turn in. *I'll just sleep in one of the bunk beds up here. Any calls come in I'll be sure to hear them.* He felt comfortable with that thought as the desk phone was only ten feet from his head. Sam dropped into the lower bunk and stared at the loft's exposed beams and rafters. *I'm off tomorrow … finally. Maybe after church I'll head down to the lower boat launch to bullshit with some of the fishermen for a while … take the boys with me. We can plink some cans with the sligshots.* Sam was asleep.

The morning sun shone thru the two skylights in Sam's loft. He awoke when the warm, golden rays crossed his face. He sat up in the bunk, still in his Class C uniform, and glanced at his watch. *7:00 … morning already. Okay … no calls. Gotta get out of these duds and into some regular jeans, get some breakfast, grab the kids, and get down to the river … See what's going on.*

Sam liked to get up and get going on the weekends. Going down to the lower boat launch was one of his favorite pass times either just to gaze out at the river, walk the river paths, or just spend time talking with fishermen launching or trailering their boats. If he could get any of his kids to come with him, all the better. It was his way of doing the things he liked do without disrupting the family schedule. He knew that when he came home he had chores to do and the obvious family responsibilities.

Sam walked into the kitchen where everyone had already started breakfast. He walked up to Peg, who was at her usual place by the stove cooking bacon and eggs. He gave her a peck on the cheek, "Morning, Honey. Mind if I take the boys with me to the lower boat launch this morning?" Peg just smiled without looking up from the frying pan. "That's fine, but remember signups for baseball are at 11:00 … and you were going to fix that gutter in the back of the house. Lawn needs raking too." Sam acknowledged the schedule then looked at his three sons seated around the large farmer style table. "Who wants to go down to the lower launch with me after breakfast? We'll take the slingshots and plink some cans." Joey was the only one interested. "I'll go Dad. I'll finally get to use my new slingshot." Matt and Steven already had plans with some friends down the road. Sam looked down at his six year old son, "Okay, pal. It's just you and me."

It was still early in the morning and the sun had yet to show itself. It seemed to be a typical April day, cloudy and cool with a chance of rain. Joey and Sam brought several tin cans to the lower boat launch where they found a secluded spot by the woods. Joey helped his dad set the cans up for target practice. Sam went back to the truck while Joey finished the job and got his slingshot out of his backpack. Out of habit, he opened the truck's door and reached in to get his portable radio off the console and clipped it to his belt. All Fish and Game Officers were required to have their radios with them even while off duty in the event of an emergency. A Fish and Game Officer's services were to be available any time, any hour, any day.

"Come on Dad. It's takin' too long. All the cans are ready." Sam came back to where Joey was waiting and they proceeded to plink the cans Joey had set up as targets. Once in a while, a fisherman or boater would notice Sam and come over to chat for a minute or two. Joey continued to shoot stones at the still upright cans. Sam was talking to one of the fishermen that had come over to say hello when he heard a radio transmission. It was from Thompson Police Dispatch to the Animal Control Officer (ACO). A train engineer passing over the Thompson trestle, south of where Sam and Joey plinked cans was reporting an injured dog below the tracks. Evidently the dog had been hit by the preceding train unbeknownst to that engineer. The reporting engineer of the second train had no choice but to pass over the injured dog again. He assured Dispatch the dog was still alive but injured and that no further damage could be done since the dog had fallen to the trestle's hurricane deck (a loose, scaffolded, maintenance deck just below the railroad tracks) and was out of the way of the train.

Sam stepped away from Joey and told him to keep practicing. He continued to listen to the radio transmissions between the ACO and several police cruisers that had arrived at the scene. It seemed as if there was some delay in getting the dog off the trestle. Sam turned his radio down and walked up to Joey, "Come on, let's go over to the train trestle. There's a dog on it that needs some help." Joey's eyes went wide, "We're going on a rescue, Dad?" "Maybe. You sit next to me in the truck and listen to the police scanner and tell me if anything comes up." Joey's face was all smiles. He reached down and put on Sam's Class B baseball cap – backwards. "Can I turn on the red flashing light, Dad?" "No, not yet, Joe. We don't know the situation yet." Joey strapped on his seat belt and acted official.

On the way to the train trestle, Sam called Peg on his cell phone. Peg answered, "Yessss?" "Honey, it appears we have a dog stranded on the train trestle south of the lower boat launch ... and it's injured. Doesn't look like anyone is making an attempt on the dog so I'm checking it out." Peg replied quickly, "But you have Joey with you. Do not leave him alone while you go do whatever you're going to do!" Sam calmly replied, "That's why I'm calling. Can you meet us down there? I'll park below the trestle so he can't see anything. I don't even know if they're going to need me yet." There was an uncomfortable pause, then Peg answered, "Okay, I'll be right there but don't leave him with anyone." Sam rolled his eyes, "I won't. I'll wait for you before I get out of the truck."

Peg got to the trestle in record time. "Hope you didn't speed, Honey," as he raised his eyebrows. Peg gave Sam a dirty look, grabbed Joey from the front seat and headed for the family van. "Hey Mom, where we goin'," Joey protested. "I'm helpin' dad with a rescue." Peg strapped Joey into the back seat of the van and said, "He's got all the help he needs now. You did your job. He's got cops and the dog warden to help him now." She turned back to Sam, waved and took Joey home.

Sam climbed up the railroad berm next to the trestle and walked onto the tracks. He saw several police cruisers parked all over the empty lot that went right up to the river's edge. At the end of the lot was a sheer cliff that dropped to the water about thirty feet. Near the cliff's edge stood a gaggle of police officers and the ACO. One of the cops saw Sam coming and announced his arrival. "Hey, Moody's here. Maybe he'll do it." Sam walked up to the group. "Anything I can do to help?" The ACO, George Tillman turned and looked Moody in the eyes. "Hey, Sam it's Sunday. Fish and Game is off duty today." Sam ignored the comment and asked, "Where is the dog?" One of the cops pointed out toward the middle of the trestle. "Right about mid river, Sam. See the little black lump out there?" Sam focused on the train trestle's mid span - the river's widest point, and saw the dog. It lay motionless on the deck just below the tracks, above the raging current by about twenty feet. Sam looked back at the group, "Well, who's going out to get him?" One of the cops was defensive, "Hey, not me. I'm one year to retirement. No one's going to get me on that trestle with that high, fast water under it." Another officer offered, "No life jackets around either, Sam. It's beyond our scope of responsibility." Sam was flabbergasted. He looked around at the remaining officers. They either turned their back to him or looked away. Finally, Sam asked the ACO, "And you, George?" "Look I'm sixty-five years old and retiring in June. I'm not risking my life for some dog." Sam started to get angry, "Fine. I'm going. Do you have anything for me to carry him back with?" The ACO said, "Sam don't be silly. It's just a dog … don't even know if he's still alive." Sam answered in an almost demanding tone, "Look, any dog that gets run over by a train, not once … but twice … and survives, deserves to live." Still no one moved. Sam raised his voice, "Get me something to carry him with. Now!" The ACO hurried to his truck and returned with a metal stretcher. He handed it to Sam, "Be careful, Sam." Sam paused as he took the stretcher and shook his head from side to side in a disapproving manner. He ran down the berm to his truck, grabbed his issue PFD (life jacket) from the cab, and headed for the entrance to the trestle.

Just before Sam went out on the trestle he turned back to the group of officers, "Has anyone called National Track Service to stop any trains that might be heading our way?" No one seemed to know. Sam pulled his radio from his belt, "419 to Headquarters." Dispatch replied immediately, "Go ahead, Sam." Sam keyed his radio, "Officer on the gauge. Stop any train traffic approaching from either direction, Thompson Train Trestle, Connecticut River." "Roger, 419," came the reply.

Sam began walking the tracks and crossed over onto the beginning of the train trestle. He walked between the gauge, or in laymen terms, tracks. The trestle was anchored to the river bank's cliff by a huge concrete slab, or headwall, embedded in the cliff wall. The headwall also acted as support for the end of the iron trestle.

When the tracks came to the trestle's headwall, Sam noticed there was nothing but air between the railroad ties. On the down river side of the gauge was a narrow catwalk made of metal. It was perforated to let the rain and snow fall through to the river below. The catwalk was no more than twelve inches wide.

Sam walked out over the river and began to leave the headwall behind him. He could see the fast, cold water thirty feet below. The higher water always resulted in a faster, angrier current. He paused for a moment to zip his PFD and clipped his belt badge to a plastic ring that hung on the left breast of the life jacket. Sam began walking the ties again, picking his steps very carefully along the ties. Suddenly, He heard a shout from the edge of the cliff he had just left. "Sam! Hold up. I'm coming with you." It was the ACO. Sam didn't know if his actions had embarrassed the Animal Control Officer into doing his duty but now watched as the ACO strapped on a spare life jacket one of the cops had dug out of his cruiser.

Sam shouted over the river's noise, "Only if you're comfortable." The ACO didn't respond. He just kept walking and soon he was out past the headwall. Sam saw him falter then stop. The older officer was not surefooted and seemed to get more uncoordinated as he tried to walk the ties. Sam walked back to him and stopped right in front of him. "George, if you're going to do this you can't look down at the water. The moving water under the trestle will cause you to lose your balance." The older officer kept looking down, "Sam, I'm froze up. Can't move. Help me." Sam turned and looked at the little black heap that still lay out on the tracks then back at the ACO. He screamed at George, "George, look at me. We have to move. The dog is suffering out there and there are trains on both sides of the river waiting for us to clear the trestle." Still the ACO remained in a frozen state. He couldn't get his arms or legs to move. Sam shouted into the man's face, "Now, George! Walk!" The older man seemed to be trying then Sam screamed at him again. "Now, George! Do it now! Look at my face!" Sam's voice was full of confidence and daring. He had to instill some strength into the frightened man. If he didn't, he'd have to save a fellow officer and somehow get him back to the headwall fifty feet away. Meanwhile, the dog out on the tracks waited. Still no movement.

After a few minutes of Sam speaking in the most reassuring tone he could muster, the ACO said, "Okay, Okay. I got it. I can keep moving." Sam was looking into the ACO's face. "Are you sure George? We have to cover about five hundred yards like this. Tell me now." "Yeah, yeah, I got it." Sam, still looking into the man's eyes said, "George … You walk on the catwalk and keep your eyes on the small of my back. You'll still be able to see the catwalk in your peripheral."

The ACO replied, "Okay, Sam I will." Sam turned to start walking out to the dog again. "We're going slow, George. Pick each step."

The two officers, one fish and game officer and one animal control officer (for domestic animal service) slowly made their way out to the stricken dog. Sam got George set in a safe position kneeling down on the catwalk and holding onto one of the track's rails, while he prepared to climb down to the hurricane deck five feet below. He looked down between the tracks and saw the dog was a young black lab about one year old. It lay on its left side on loose planking that rested on thin metal supports attached to the structure above. The supports formed a "U" that the planking rested on. The dog's right rear leg had been severed halfway down just above the knee and was dangling in the open air above the water rushing by twenty feet below. The only thing that still kept the leg attached was a little strand of fur that had not yet been cut.

Sam reached the dog and knelt down beside him on the rickety platform. *That poor dog must be in so much pain! As soon as I grab him he's going to want to bite.* Sam paused for a moment. *Can't worry about that now. Just have to get him topside and back to shore. Don't know how much longer George can hang in there.* Sam looked into the dog's sad eyes. It was as if the dog was saying … 'please help me.' *Here goes,* Sam said to himself and reached for the dog. He was careful to keep the dog in a horizontal position with no quick movements so as to keep the strand of fur from tearing. If the fur tore now he would lose the leg to the rushing current below and all hopes of reattaching the leg would be lost.

Sam stood up with the dog in his arms and had to raise it above his head to get it to the tracks where he had left the stretcher. "George, can you grab the dog? I can't lift him any higher because of the way I'm standing." "Can't move from this spot, Sam. Sorry. I'm not letting go of the tracks." Sam knew he was on his own. One false step with the dog's weight and they were both going for a swim. He took a couple of deep breaths and with one great effort lifted the dog higher and at arm's length, while moving his supporting leg to a spot above the hurricane deck's platform. It wouldn't have been such a hard lift had he not had to keep the dog so far out in front of his own body.

Sam let the dog down gently on the stretcher above and in front of him and the dog stayed where Sam placed him. Sam let go of his purchase on the hurricane deck and grabbed one of the track's rails, now at his chest level and pulled himself up. He rolled over onto his back next to the dog and caught his breath. It was only then that Sam felt the cold April wind blowing across his sweat soaked body. He turned his head to the right and looked at George, "You okay George?" George didn't look up but said, "For now … but I need to get out of here." Sam sat up, "Okay we're leaving. Stand up slowly facing the way we came. You grab one side of the stretcher and I'll take the other. Stay on the catwalk. I'll walk the ties."

The two officers began their walk back to the river's bank. George had one end of the stretcher and Sam the other. As they continued toward shore, Sam noticed George was moving faster and faster. George was beginning to panic again. It was becoming harder and harder for Sam to accurately place his lead foot on the next railroad tie. "Alright, George slow down a bit. I know you want to get back but it's a hell of a lot easier walking that catwalk you're on than it is out here on the ties."

George ignored Sam and kept increasing the pace. Sam shouted to George above the river below, "George. You're getting reckless. Stop for a minute." Finally George stopped. "George, we have to work together or we're going to dump the dog into the river. I don't have anything out here but air between the ties. We have to coordinate our movement." The older officer took his eyes off the catwalk. "Sorry, Sam. I'm starting to lose it again." Sam kept George in an eye lock. "Okay George, you're doing great. Just slow it down. Can you feel me on the end of this stretcher?" George nodded that he did. Sam continued in an almost soothing tone, "Okay, let's start walking again and try to walk with me. Feel my movement on the stretcher." The ACO nodded in compliance and they continued toward the shoreline.

The three-some; dog, ACO and Sam crossed over the headwall and onto solid ground. The ACO made it obvious he was going to put his end of the stretcher down immediately. Sam felt the movement and lowered his end also. The ACO kept his head down and headed for his truck where he could be alone and get through his embarrassment. Sam looked back down at the dog who hadn't taken his eyes off him for the whole trip. "Everything's is going to be okay boy." His voice was low and soothing. "Sam stroked the dog's head and continued to speak to the injured dog, "It's okay … You're gonna' be okay, boy. We're going to get you to the animal hospital. You're going to be okay."

It was as if a bond had formed between the two. The waiting patrolmen rushed up onto the track's berm to where Sam knelt beside the dog. Someone backed up the ACO's truck to where they could safely place the dog and stretcher for transport to the hospital. One of the cops went to shut the double doors at the back of the truck and Sam caught the door and held it open. He yelled to the front where the ACO sat, "Hey, George … Can you hear me?" George nodded in compliance. Sam looked around at the other officers now all huddled at the back of the ACO's truck. "I want the dog. He's got no tags and if no one claims him in twenty-four hours he's mine. I'll pay for the reattachment or the amputation." He looked around at all the sullen faces. "Anybody have anything to say about that?" No one said a word. Sam slammed the door to the back of the truck and slapped it with his hand twice and the truck left for the animal hospital with the ACO, dog and driver. Sam headed for his truck.

★ ★ ★ ★

Chapter 9

Monday morning found the Thompson Fish and Game Department at roll call once again. Lieutenant Alban lined out the day's activities for each patrol and gave specific instructions for what the prime area of focus was for today. Before he brought the meeting to an end he made mention of the dog's rescue on the train trestle. "We had another rescue yesterday at the Thompson Train trestle." It appears there were several on duty policemen, including the Animal Control Officer on scene. One of our men, Marine Patrol Officer Moody, was off duty at the time and also the one to make the save." There was a slight pause as Alban looked up at Sam and smiled. It was the first friendly gesture from Alban since the New Hampshire incident. The roll call room came alive with the room's applause. Corporal Frank Beech was sitting in a kind of slumped position on the far end of the room. "That's my Golden Boy," he said smiling while nodding his head. "Way to go, Sammy."

Sam just sat in his place in the back corner of the room and raised his right hand slightly in acknowledgement of the attention. Pat James and Tom Stafford, who were sitting closest to Sam, playfully slapped him on the arms and pushed on the back of his shoulders.

Alban continued, "Officer Moody was off duty gentlemen." He stopped and looked around the room for effect. "He was spending some time with his son at the boat launch when he heard the call on his portable (portable radio). I keep telling you guys to bring that thing with you wherever you go, even when you're off duty. If Sam had not done that, the rescue would never have happened and a one year old black lab would be history." Someone spoke up, "Excuse me LT … I thought you said there were cops and the ACO on scene." Alban replied, "There was. Actually, there were six police officers and the ACO. They had refused to go out on the trestle because of the extreme river conditions." Alban stopped and looked at Moody again, this time in a more serious way. "It took guts and a sincere feeling for why we wear these badges to do what he did. It took a game warden." Alban straightened up and addressed the room of wardens. "Everyone on their feet and stand at attention." Everyone immediately came to their feet and assumed the position. Alban was deadpan serious, "Marine Patrol Officer Samuel Moody … front and center." Sam walked to the front of the room and stood before the lieutenant. Alban looked directly into Sam's eyes, "You made us proud son. You made me proud. You reacted to a terrible situation and without any thought for yourself, and carried out your responsibilities flawlessly. It was text book. Well done, Sam." With that Alban reached out to shake Sam's hand and with the other hand gave Sam a gold rimmed railroad pin and two corporal stripes. Alban raised his arm in a salute and Sam saluted him back. "Yeah Sammy," someone shouted. The ceremony over and the room broke into huge applause and catcalls. Alban dropped his salute, bent over and whispered into Sam's ear, "Welcome back, son. Good job." Alban turned and left the room without another word.

Sam was flabbergasted. He just stood at Alban's podium holding the pin and the stripes. The other wardens surrounded him and congratulated their comrade. Tom and Pat just stood at the back of the room and smiled as their buddy had his moment of fame. Once the room started thinning out, Tom and Pat joined Sam and walked him out of the room. Pat walked with his hand on Moody's shoulder, "Looks like you're back in the admin's favor again, Sam. Good for you." Tom just smiled and shook Sam's hand. The three went straight to the cafeteria for a celebratory coffee before going their separate ways.

As the three wardens sat and talked about what just happened, Tom Stafford who had been relatively quiet until now spoke up. "Sam, I don't mean to put a damper on things but do you think the stripes and Alban's attitude has anything to do with the fact that you showed up all the other departments with that rescue?" Sam looked confused, "What do you mean, Tom?" Stafford went on, "I mean one week ago Alban handed you, Sawyer, and Smalls your asses in a basket over that capsized boat rescue and the response times and how bad it made us look as first responders to other departments. Here, you had the cops worried about falling in, the ACO scared shitless that he wouldn't make it to retirement, and … the fire department didn't even offer mutual aid." Sam looked shocked again, "I wasn't even thinking about …," Stafford cut him off, "We know, Sam. You just reacted as you or anyone of us would have but that's what redeemed our position as first responders." Sam shook his head in understanding. "Yeah, makes sense, Tom. But you know what? I have to go check on that dog. If no one claims him he's mine." He bid his friends farewell and left for the Marine Division's office.

Sam hung up the phone with the animal hospital with a concerned look. Corporal Sawyer sat across from Sam and had listened to the whole conversation. "Well, what's the verdict Sam? Is he yours or what?" Sam looked up at John and smiled, "They had to amputate the entire right rear leg but he's doing fine. Being so young it shouldn't affect him in any way … just appearance." Sawyer looked across the desk at Sam, "I can't believe you're going to adopt a three-legged dog," and shook his head. Sam shot back, "Hey, John … any dog gets run over by two trains and lives deserves a good life." Sawyer just shrugged his shoulders and turned a little red.

Sam added, "To answer your question … No one claimed him so he's mine." Sam was happy. He sat back in the desk chair and nodded his head favorably. Sawyer smiled and asked, "What're you gonna' call him?" "Been thinking about that. I'm going to call him Traveller. Traveller was the name of Civil War General, Robert E. Lee's horse. Went everywhere with him and was very much in tune with the General. Seemed to be able to anticipate each other. The way I see it, this dog came looking for me. As soon as I looked into his eyes on that trestle I felt there was something different about him." Sam paused a moment, looked up at the ceiling, smiled and said, "Yeah … that's my dog … Traveller."

★ ★ ★ ★

CHAPTER 10

The two Marine Corporals, Sam and John, sat in the marine division's office and talked for a while. They shared one large desk, set up so they could sit directly across from one another. The marine office was small compared to what Captain Fletcher and Lieutenant Alban enjoyed but it was comfortable and functional. Sam took the extra time to read into more of the Hanks accident and write down some of the more important clues and leads into a notebook he kept locked in the top drawer of the desk.

Presently the phone rang, "Marine Division … Sawyer here." The corporal's voice was without emotion and monotone. Sam looked up but went back to his writing. Then he heard Sawyer say, "Oh you want to speak to Officer Moody? Oh, okay. Just a minute, Maam." Sawyer handed the phone to Sam sitting across the desk, "For you, Sam. It's a woman but it's not Peg." Sam raised his eyebrows and took the phone, "Moody here. What can I do for you?" Sawyer hadn't looked away from Sam yet and noticed his facial expression had gone from plain and unassuming to focused attention. Sam leaned forward in the chair and his demeanor became that of concern. "Oh, you're here in the station? Okay, sure … I'll meet you in the lobby."

Sam rose from the chair and looked at Sawyer. "She's here in the station. It's Helen Woodruff. You know, Jake's girl friend from New Hampshire? She owned the land Jake was poaching on." Sawyer sat up straight in his chair. "What does she want?" "Don't know yet … wants to talk to me … alone." Sawyer stood up and grabbed Sam by the arm, "Do you want me to come? You may need someone to witness the conversation." Sam shrugged off Sawyer's hand, "Nah, I'm good. Thanks though." Sam started for the door. Sawyer said in a low tone, "Be careful what you say, Sam. You don't know what she's after." Sam closed the office door and started for the lobby.

Helen Woodruff sat on one end of a long couch in the Thompson Police Department's lobby. Her small frame made the couch look larger than it was. She sat bolt upright and stared straight ahead as if she was concentrating hard on something. Sam had only met her once and that was during the court proceedings that followed the attack on the poacher's camp in New Hampshire last year. Although she owned the land that Jake and the poachers used, it had been confirmed she had no knowledge of what they were doing or what their intentions were. Sam's attack on the camp was considered police business and required no permission from the owner.

Sam could see her through the glass door that led to the lobby. *Is that why she's here*, he thought. *Is she going to try and sue the department for turning her little meadow in the woods into a battlefield?* Sam stopped before he walked through the door and took a deep breath. *Don't anticipate. Just do it.*

Sam pushed through the double doors and smiled at the woman. He walked up to Helen and put his hand out to shake hers, "Hello, Ms. Woodruff. It's nice to see you again. What brings you to Connecticut?" Helen offered no hand,

"Call me, Helen." She remained seated and continued, "Officer, Moody. This is not a social visit. I came here for two reasons. One … is to ask you a question and the other is to find out where Jake is." Sam took his hand back and said, "What is your question, Helen?" Helen stared at Sam for a good minute before speaking, then stood up and looked Sam right in the eyes. "Who do you think you are … or were? You come up to New Hampshire … out of your jurisdiction and unprovoked and you get involved in something that was none of your business." Sam started to answer but she cut him off, "Jake and I were developing a nice little life on that farm. It was as if I had a family all over again, then you come in with guns and police cars, tear up my property, and turn it into a battle zone." Again Sam started to intervene. Helen put her hand up to protest. "Let me finish, sonny." She stepped toward Sam, "Yes, you took all that away. Don't you realize we have our own woods–cops up there … and they're probably better than you too." Helen paused to catch her breath. She seemed to be getting angrier with every sentence. "Part of me wants to thank you for stopping Jake and what he was doing to me and all the poor animals on my property. The other part of me hates you for helping to end my second chance to be happy and to have companionship."

Sam just relegated himself to hear out Helen. No one had even considered how the whole New Hampshire incident affected her. After a moment, Helen continued, "I'm not stupid, Officer Moody. I know that Jake was using me and my land for his own purposes … and he would have probably left me after he was done with what my land could offer him." Helen paused again, then said, "I was so happy. What I didn't know wasn't going to hurt me … and now I have nothing." Helen started to cry. Sam stepped forward and put an arm around her slouched shoulders. Helen leaned into Sam and rested her head on his chest. "It's okay, Helen. I understand completely. Just know he will never be able to take advantage of you or your property again. Your property will be watched over for as long as you own it. That was something your own New Hampshire officials offered."

Helen lifted her head from Sam's chest and took a step back. She straightened up, cleared her throat, and looked into Sam's eyes again. "Okay, I've said my piece. Now, for the second question. Where is Jake Farmer? I want to talk to him too." Sam said he would ask his superiors if that was possible and if she could wait a few moments he'd come back with some information.

Sam stood in his familiar spot in front of Lieutenant Alban's desk. "Why does she want to see him Sam? It's been several months since the incident and court case. Why now?" Sam replied, "Well they were living together, LT. It was an adult relationship and Farmer hasn't been able to get out of bed except for the necessary requirements. She looks pretty harmless sir." Finally Alban agreed, "Yeah, I guess we can't deny her in this case. Make sure she doesn't have anything on her and escort her to the rehab center." "Okay, LT. I'll give her the news."

Sam led Helen to the Thompson Rehabilitation and Development Center in his marine department cruiser. He pulled into the parking lot and parked closest to the entrance and Helen parked right next to him. Sam got out of the cruiser and opened the door to Helen's car and helped her out. "Okay, Officer Moody. Thank you. I'll be doing this on my own thank you." Sam looked at Helen with a questioning look, "Do what on your own, Helen? I thought you just came by for a visit." Helen replied, "I mean I'm a grown woman who can handle a whole farm on her own without help from any man, so I sure as hell can visit an old man lying in bed … without assistance." Sam smiled down at the aging woman. *What a sweetheart. He must have really hurt her. Why did someone like this have to get involved with Jake Farmer?* Helen stared Sam in the eyes again. "Well, go on. I said thank you. Now be on your way." Sam tipped his Stetson at her and bid her a good day.

Helen waited at the Rehab's entrance until Sam's cruiser was out of sight. She turned and looked up at the sign over the entrance, *Rehab facility. All this time and still in rehab. Must have been worse than I thought.* Helen let the slightest hint of a wicked little smile cross her lips. *Serves the bastard right.*

Former Fish and Game Warden Jake Farmer sat propped up in his hospital bed watching television. A new nurse came in and informed him it was time for his mid-day oxygen treatment. Jake let the young nurse fuss around his prone position in the bed and admired every bit of the young female's attributes. "Now don't pull it out this time," the nurse urged. "When you can stop pulling the ventilator out, we'll be able to untie your wrist straps." The straps were attached to Jake's wrists and to the associated bed rails. Apparently, Jake's heart attack was so massive that it had affected several of his bodily functions. He had been without air for so long in the meadow on the night of the attack, part of the brain responsible sending some of the involuntary messages to specific parts of his body was affected. One of these was the signal to his lungs for continuous breathing.

The nurse left and Jake started to settle down again. His favorite game show had just started so he began to breathe easier. The first commercial came on and there was a knock on the door. Jake shifted his eyes to the door and watched it open. Helen Woodruff walked in and stood at the foot of Jake's bed. He couldn't say anything or raise his bound arms so he tried to speak with his eyes. He raised his eyebrows to indicate surprise and nodded his head. Helen spoke quietly at first, "Relax Jake. This won't take long." She looked around the room and saw the oxygen tank, ventilator, and oxygen flow apparatus. She slowly walked over to it and stood next to it. Jake followed her movement around the bed with his eyes. She looked at the oxygen tank and then back at Jake. "You son of a bitch. You rotten son of a bitch! How could you have misled me in so many ways? Why would you prey on someone who had already been handed a terrible consequence?" Jake just rolled his eyes and motioned with his head for her to leave. "Oh you want me to leave … so soon? I don't think so, Mister. Not till I'm done with you." Jake showed anger in his face and he started to squint his eyes. Helen looked up at the heart monitor that was positioned above Jake's bed. His blood pressure was beginning to climb. "Look at yourself … lying in bed. Mr. big tough game warden turned poacher. Not so big now are you? You can't even stand on your own two feet without gasping for air. Well, you're no game warden any more … don't even have a pension any more. You lost it all big boy." Helen watched the monitor as Jake's blood pressure rose, even faster now. "It was all for nothing you lying son of a bitch. You have nothing left Jakey boy … NOTHING! If you get better, and I mean if … you're going straight to prison for a couple of years. Your life is over … Jakey." Helen's voice was getting louder as she spoke. "When I think of how I let you sweet talk your way into my house that morning … how I trusted you and everything you said." Helen paused to catch her breath. "I can't even believe myself!"

Helen reached over to the oxygen tank and placed her hand on the tank's flow control valve. Jake watched Helen's every move now. He began to show some discomfort. Helen could see beads of sweat as they formed on his forehead. She placed her hand on top of the valve and slid it along the surface, "You've always had to be the one in control, haven't you? Even when you weren't supposed to be in control, you fixed it so you really were." Helen took her hand off the valve, made two fists with her arms bent, "You lying, cheating bastard." She brought her right hand back down and rested it on the oxygen flow control valve again. "You caused me to betray the loving memory of my dear deceased husband … and let me tell you asshole … he was more a man than you in every way." Helen looked up at the heart monitor. It was starting to blink on and off. "Here's a change old man. Now I'm in charge." Helen tightened her grip on the valve and she flexed her fingers so Jake could see them move on the valve. Jake's blood pressure was approaching the warning level. Jake began shaking his head in a side to side manner. "Yeah, Jake. All I have to do is turn the valve and unplug the monitor so it doesn't alarm … and then you're done. No one will even know 'till they come to change your bed sheets in the morning."

Helen could see the desperation in Jake's eyes. It was a pleading look – his head shaking from side to side. Jake was experiencing the greatest fear he had ever known all caused by a frail little women of sixty years old. Helen looked up at the monitor. *Looks like it's about to go off,* and removed her hand from the valve. She reached over the bed and slapped Jake across the face, "Bastard!"

Helen turned and walked out the door. She felt a smile cross her face as she continued down the hallway. A feeling she had not experienced in six months. Her pace was deliberate and steady. As she neared the nurse's station just before the rehab's exit, she heard an alarm and stepped to the side of the long hallway as three nurses and a doctor raced by pushing a crash cart in the direction from which she just came. Helen never looked back. She pushed through the double entry doors and raised a hand in the air with her middle digit pointing to the sky.

★ ★ ★ ★

CHAPTER 11

The month of May arrived with the usual accoutrements. Buds on the trees that had been struggling to make an appearance all through April were now beginning to show themselves. The sun seemed brighter and higher in the sky and the flora was beginning to bloom. Everything was getting greener and generally happier. The air felt warmer and became breezier but more tolerable than it had been through the previous months. Summer was finally on the way.

Sam stood in his favorite spot on his cabin's farmer style porch. It was early morning and he sipped his hot, black coffee in solitude as he waited for the honkers to make their annual flyover. He stood by the railing and leaned against one of the porch posts. It was his favorite time of the day where everything was simple and clear … and quiet. Sam kept his gaze skyward as he closed his eyes and let the new morning sun warm his face. He tried to block out all immediate thoughts and concentrate on sounds the conscious mind normally ignores.

Eventually he allowed some of the more welcome thoughts to enter his consciousness. He began to think of his new dog Traveller, and what a welcome addition he'd made to the family so far. Traveller was healing rapidly and getting attached to the family as much as the Moodys were getting attached to him. Traveller was beginning to limp around the house and was learning the house rules very quickly. The kids loved their new pet and didn't seem to realize he only had three legs. To them he was the best dog they had ever seen.

Sam had left the screen door open to the kitchen and knew Traveller was inside laying by the fridge. He turned his head and whistled. It was a long blow followed by two short ones. After only a month Traveller had picked up on the call and was responding nicely. The screen door swung open and a three legged black lab came hobbling out of the kitchen. Sam smiled and the dog dutifully came over, sat down and leaned against Sam's supporting leg. "Good boy, Traveller. You'll be going on patrol with me in no time pal." Sam reached down and patted Traveller's upturned head.

Sam glanced at his watch, drained the coffee cup, and left it on the porch rail. "Come on, boy. Got to go to work." Sam ushered the dog back into the house and began collecting his things for work. "Where will you be working today, Honey," Peg asked as Sam walked by the sink … one of Peg's usual spots. Sam replied without looking, "We have river training on the new boat today. We'll be in the stretch either side of the upper boat launch area. It's just a work boat and smaller than the Carolina … no big deal. Have to get the feel of it and where everything is on it. The whole department will be there except for one patrol that will be on uniformed duty in one of the cruisers."

Now ready to leave, Sam gave Peg a quick peck on the cheek on his way out the door. Peg answered with, "Have a good day and be careful. Remember no hero stuff." She smirked.

Yeah, like he heard that, and shook her head. Sam was already out the door and heading for his truck.

The drive to the boathouse was the usual, enjoyable twenty minutes through some of Thompson's finest scenery. It always gave Sam some time to think and plan his day. *I think it's time to approach Alban about investigating Hanks' murder. I'm in good standing with him right now and after all, it is one of the unsolved cases in the department. Maybe I'll initiate a conversation after practice today.*

Sam drove past the boathouse and right to the boat launch. Sawyer and Smalls had already retrieved the new boat and had it beached on the sand next to the new dock. It was a small workboat, of the Jonboat class. Flat bottomed with a steel hull and squared off bow and stern. Sawyer was loading PFDs and general patrol apparatus into her for the days practice. Most of the department was there and milled around the beach until Smalls was ready to begin the training.

Sam jumped down from his truck and threw open one side of his truck box to get his PFD. Stafford and James pulled into the launch's lower parking lot. They also retrieved their PFDs and walked over to Sam. "Hey Buddy." Stafford reached out and gave Sam a slap on the back. James just smiled and nodded at Sam. Stafford leaned in closer to Sam and spoke quietly, "Did you get to speak to Alban about investigating Hanks yet?" Sam just smirked and shook his head to indicate he had not. He let a moment go by then said, "Today. After practice I'll go in and talk to him." Stafford straightened up and let out a small sigh. "Okay, but just so you know I'm not getting involved until you clear it with him ... Okay?" Sam shot Stafford a serious look, "Tom!?" Pat James interrupted before Tom could answer, "Me too, Sam. Got to be up front this time. I want to get off nights sometime soon, and that means no more standing in front of Alban's desk listening to him rant and rave." Sam stood and stared at his two old friends and shook his head in affirmance. He understood where they were coming from and also knew they were protecting him as well as themselves. "I intend to speak to him guys … just haven't had the time or opportunity." They just shook their heads as if they understood. Sam changed the subject, "Let's go take a look at the new boat." The three wardens started for the Jonboat beached on the sand.

Practice on the new workboat went by fairly quickly. It consisted mostly of listening to Smalls talk about the boat as it lay on the beach and the discussion of certain items and where they lay in the boat. There was a little about the new engine but nothing the wardens hadn't seen before. Before it was over, Smalls made each warden pair up with another warden and take the new craft for a spin on the water.

"Okay guys," Smalls addressed the entire group. "That's it. Practice is over. Sign these marine certifications to say you have attended the class and are now able to operate the new boat." As the men milled around looking for a flat place to look over the documents and sign their names, Sam got Stafford's attention. Stafford finally noticed Sam and gave him a questioning look. Sam nodded his head as if to say 'over there by the Jonboat's tow vehicle.' The two men nonchalantly walked over to the boat. Stafford spoke first. "What's up?" Sam was looking out at the river. "You're off today, right?" "Yeah … why," Stafford was curious. Sam began, "I heard what you said before practice and I understand, but this is a perfect opportunity to take the new boat upriver and get a look at that marina that houses all those Checkmates … You know … Speed Dreamers. Let them know we're going to be watching right off the bat this season." Stafford looked mildly perturbed. "Sam, I meant what I said earlier." Sam quickly put in, "I know you did but you'll just be there as a passenger. I'm driving." Stafford just stared at Sam a minute. Sam added, "I'm not going to do anything today anyway. Just going to do a slow drive-by. Promise." Stafford finally agreed as long as it was just a 'go and see' patrol.

The group of wardens on the beach began to break up. It was Sunday so most of the Unit was off for the day. Sam saw that Smalls was preparing to put the Jonboat back in the water to get it on the trailer for transport back to the boat house. Sam shouted to Smalls, "Hey, Sarge. I'll take care of that. Do you mind if Stafford and I take it upstream. We'll do a little patrol, break in the new engine, then bring it back to the boathouse." Smalls was taken back a little. "It's Sunday Sam. You're off for the rest of the day." Sam put in quickly, "Yeah I know but the wife and kids are going to be out for a while and I'd rather do this than go home to an empty house." Smalls shrugged his shoulders, "Yeah, go ahead. Don't get into trouble with this boat. It's just a workboat, Sam. No speed, still light on lines and safety equipment and Sawyer forgot to bring the anchor because it was supposed to be a beach demonstration only." Sam smiled, "You got it, Sarge. Just going to take her for a ride." Smalls nodded his head as he walked away.

Sam and Tom Stafford pushed the Jonboat out into the river stern first and left the bow beached on the sand. One at a time, they hopped in from the bow to keep from getting their boots wet. Tom came back to the stern, just behind Sam's position at the helm (amidships on the starboard side) and tipped the outboard into the water. A warden standing by pushed them off the beech once the new Johnson outboard came to life. Tom stumbled back up to the bow to balance the weight in the boat and Sam nudged the throttle forward to start the boat upriver for their so called drive-by.

The boat's radio system had not yet been hooked up so Sam keyed his portable, "419 and 422 in the workboat enroute to Mass line." "Roger 419," came the reply from Dispatch. Sam and Tom went through the usual obstacle course which meant avoiding whirlpools around the old piers, negotiating the narrow channel, and the struggle to keep the prop in deep water without letting the river's current get the advantage.

Channel negotiation was a little harder in the workboat than it was in the Carolina because of the manual tilt engine. There was no power tilt adjust as there was in the Carolina. The first mate would have to manually tilt the engine up by grabbing the engine cowling on both sides and move the prop upward and clear of any obstruction. Fortunately, today had been a heavy water day because of recent rains and there was plenty of water in the channel.

As Sam and Tom passed the peninsula, Sam nodded to Tom, "Mass line coming up. Hold on, I'm going to open her up." As soon as Stafford got comfortable in the bow Sam pushed his throttle all the way forward and the little work boat pointed to the sky first and then settled out on plane again. It was a rougher ride than the bigger and heavier Carolina but the new engine scooted them across the surface at a quick 15 knots. Sam felt the roughness and the stiffer steering. *Not bad speed for a workboat but she's pretty tight in the steerage category.*

The two wardens on their day off skimmed the river's surface toward the Massachusetts line. Soon the Jonboat passed over the border and Sam angled her over toward the river's east bank making sure to stay about one hundred feet off the shoreline. For the next five minutes there was nothing but trees and scrub brush along the river's edge. Finally, some cottages could be seen through the trees tethered to docks in the river by a well-worn path through the forest that separated them. Sam slowed the Jonboat to about one half of throttle. The little workboat rode smoother and quieter and allowed a better view of the shore line as they motored by.

Tom sat in the bow with his feet on the front of the squared front and watched upstream through his binoculars. "Sam, we have one marina coming up … about two o'clock starboard side." Sam looked in the direction and the marina was almost hidden by some small islands that sat out in front of it. There appeared to be some boaters trying to get their boats in the water and others that had already docked for the season, fussing with deck lines and water hoses. Tom talked as he looked through the binoculars, "No Checkmates yet Sam, just some regular size outboards, a few bass boats, and a couple of those pontoon party boats."

Now and then a boater would look up and see the little Jonboat that carried two uniformed game wardens and smile. The feeling from the general public was that if there was a uniformed officer in the boat there should also be some indication of speed. *Good*, Sam thought. *No one is going to suspect us looking for anything in this slow little work boat.* Suddenly, "Hey Sam. There it is … Speed Dreamers. About five hundred yards ahead, one o'clock starboard." Sam couldn't see anything at that distance and the glare off the water was particularly bad this time of day. Sam asked, "See a small shack or anything to the right or left of the marina, like an outdoor restaurant? We're looking for Joey's Speed Trap." Tom adjusted his binoculars, "There is something under those willow trees hanging out over the river to the right of the marina's main building." Sam shut the motor down and they began to drift. "Okay, now we know where it is. Why don't you put those binoculars away for now? Don't want to raise too much suspicion."

Sam's radio crackled to life, "Headquarters to 419." Sam keyed his mic, "Connecticut River, North." "419 you have a nineteen foot Searay, I/O type (inboard/outboard) stuck on the dam. It's sitting on the dam, bow to stern, and is in danger of going over sideways. Occupants didn't see the dam as they approached. Expedite!" Tom shouted back to Sam from the bow, "It's that low head dam problem again. No one ever sees it in time."

Sam turned on the Jonboat's ignition and spun the little work boat in as tight a one hundred eighty degree turn that it would allow, pushed the throttle forward and headed for the Thompson Dam. Sam keyed his portable, "Enroute Thompson Dam, ETA is ten minutes. Better dispatch the Carolina too. This boat isn't outfitted yet – no emergency equipment aboard." Dispatch replied, "Expedite and do what you can. Everyone has been sent home for the day so they will be responding from their homes. It's going to be a little while." *Shit*, Sam thought. *They're going to have to return and go back to the boathouse.* "419 to Dispatch. Tone the Fire Department's hovercraft."

Lieutenant Gene Alban was just sitting down to a family dinner when he heard the call on his portable radio. Usually the wardens were not required to keep their radios on when at home or off duty, but Alban was the Unit Commander and had to keep abreast of what was happening at all times. It wasn't very often that his portable or scanner was silent, on or off the job. "The Hover Craft?" Alban stood up from his chair. The rest of the family just rolled their eyes or looked down at their plates. "Why is Moody asking for the Hover Craft? We need Marine One (the Carolina) out there first." Alban was now up and out of his chair and heading for the telephone. "The Unit's on Holiday and the only thing we have in the river is that little workboat ... Damn it! We're gonna' look like shit again." Alban looked back at his family sitting around the table. "Sorry guys I have to get out there and supervise this. There will be other barbecues." The Albans were used to the drill and just nodded their heads but he was already out the door and starting his truck.

Sam and Tom were approaching the old piers by the Thompson boat launch making a straight run for the Thompson Dam. Sam glanced over at the boat launch. No emergency vehicles yet. *I may have to incorporate the use of any available boaters if department help doesn't arrive soon.* Tom looked back at Sam, "Hey Sam. What are you gonna' do when you get there? We have no tow lines, no PFDs, no anchors … nothing." "Just take it as it comes. We'll keep them company until help arrives … talk to them … make sure they don't panic and cause that boat to go over." Tom just rolled his eyes and turned back to the front of the boat.

The Jonboat passed under the new bridge and was nearing the stricken vessel on the dam. Sam slowed the boat to half throttle and stayed far enough upriver to stay out of the rip current caused by the irregular shaped dam. The dam was of the 'low head' design and was one of the most dangerous ever built. The water level above the dam was the same height as the top of the dam structure making it hard to see from a boater approaching from upriver. The term low head also referred to the height of the dam above the water below. Usually there was a three to four foot drop to the rocks below and then the rapids began. A fall straight down from that height to the rocks below could smash the boats bottom leaving the rapids to take apart any remaining parts of the hull.

Sam maneuvered the Jonboat as close as he could without endangering his own prop. The water became shallower and the current faster as it got closer to the lip of the dam. Sam turned on the blue flashing light to indicate he was a marine patrol vessel. "Tom, watch for rocks as I make a pass by their boat. Tell them to stay calm and not to move around." The stricken boat had a family on board. There was a man, a woman, and a boy of about ten years old. The father stood behind the helm and the mother sat amidships holding her son. All three looked terrified.

The noise from the dam was extremely loud and made shouting to the family pointless. Tom looked back at Sam, "They can't hear us over the noise from the dam." Sam could barely hear Tom, "Use your open hands with fingers spread apart and move them up and down. Just like a traffic cop would do when he's telling you to slow down. Just being here with them has to make them feel better." Tom made the gestures and the husband smiled back and waved his hand in the air as if to say he understood.

Sam kept the Jonboat in a figure eight pattern about thirty yards upriver of the Searay and just out of the rip current. Sam keyed his portable, "419 ... headquarters. Where is the Carolina or the Hover craft? I'm with the Searay on the dam now but can't do anything to help. If they go over, I'm going to have to try to jump the dam to pick up people before the rapids take them." Dispatch came back quick, "419 - Carolina is launching now from lower boat ramp and the Hover Craft is approaching you from downriver. Keep your position. You are authorized to jump the dam only if they go over ... Repeat, only if Searay goes over." "Sam keyed his portable, "419, Roger."

Sam kept looking upstream for any assistance. Finally, he saw the Carolina's light bar coming over the horizon. "There she is, Tom. The Carolina is just passing under the bridge now." "Who's the skipper," Tom kept his eyes on the rip current only a few yards away from the Jonboat. Sam was relieved, "It's John Sawyer." "Well that's good news," Tom was also relieved. "Here comes the Hover Craft. See her approaching from below?" Sam was happy the Hover Craft was available. If the Searay went over she would be in perfect position to pick up swimmers. Sam keyed his portable, "Marine One to Hover One." "Go ahead Marine One. You are Command. What are your instructions?" Command meant that the department in charge was responsible for the situation and was making all the decisions. Sam replied, "Hover One, stay on station one hundred feet downriver and directly behind the Searay. Standby to pick up swimmers in the event she goes over." "Roger, Marine One."

Sam looked over at the Carolina now passing between the Jonboat and the dam and keyed his portable, "Sawyer get out of there ... you're too close to the rip." Sam watched Sawyer's face. There was no reaction, no sign that Sawyer could even hear him. Tom shouted back to Sam, "I don't think he can hear the radio transmission ... or he doesn't have his radio on." Sam guided the Jonboat a little closer to the rip as the Carolina started another pass between the Jonboat and the dam. This time Sam shouted to the skipper, "John, you're too close to the rip. Get out of there." Marine Corporal John Sawyer didn't even look at Sam or Tom. He seemed transfixed on the situation. Tom shouted again, "What is he doing?" As if in answer to Tom's question, the Carolina suddenly made a sideways slip, stern first toward the dam. Sawyer tried to correct for it and gunned the Carolina's throttle but the rip current was too strong. Sam and Tom watched helplessly as the Carolina collided with the Searay pushing it and its occupants over the dam. The Searay went over and straight down to the rocks below and the Carolina came down next to her pushing her up against the waterfall. The Searay's occupants began to panic as their boat was literally being filled with water by the dam's waterfall.

Sawyer was taking on water in the Carolina too as she had caught a few rusty rebars that had been protruding from the old dam. There was a twelve inch gash in the stern's bottom on the port side and another two inch diameter hole in the floor right behind the helm. Sawyer reacted quickly and ordered his first mate to throw a line to the Searay's skipper. Since the boats were literally in contact with one another, Sawyer held the Carolina in position while his first mate lashed the two crafts together and helped them aboard the Carolina. Once everyone was aboard, Sawyer ordered the lash lines cut so he could drift free from the now swamped Searay. Clear of the dam and its waterfall, Sawyer gunned the throttle and made a controlled turn to the center of the river and got her bow pointed down river. The Carolina was still taking on water but at a slower rate due to the forward momentum of the boat, so Sawyer steered as close as possible to the east river bank and made for the lower launch.

Sam keyed his portable, "Hover One from Marine One." "Go ahead Marine One." Can you get a tow line on that swamped Searay and tow her to the lower boat launch please? We'll meet with you there. Call Dispatch for an ambulance for arrival at the lower boat launch." "Roger, Marine One. See you downriver. Hover One out."

Sam and Tom locked eyes for a moment. Sam turned the Jonboat upriver, "Let's get out of the river. There's going to be hell to pay once we get down to the lower boat launch. Alban's probably there already." Tom just shook his head, "Great … just great … and on my day off too."

★ ★ ★ ★

CHAPTER 12

All points of interest now focused on the lower boat launch which meant the two wardens had to travel back upriver to get the Jonboat back to the upper boat launch where its trailer waited. Tom and Sam worked fast to get the workboat secured for the road trip to the lower boat launch where the Searay's occupants would be arriving in the Carolina.

Other support personnel that had responded to the river accident within the last thirty minutes were also enroute to the same location, and Hover One was in the process of recovering and towing the swamped Searay and would be depositing her there also.

Sam and Tom sped to the lower boat launch, lights only, with the Jonboat safely secured to its trailer and in tow. "I wonder if the LT was listening to those radio transmissions. We looked like Keystone Cops on that one," Tom Stafford just looked out the window and shook his head. Sam kept his eyes on the road and said, "Are you kidding? Of course he heard it … and right now is probably planning on how loud he's going to ream us. He never turns that damn scanner off."

The turn came up for Bridge Lane, the access road to the lower boat launch. Sam keyed his portable, "419 and 422 enroute to Thompson Lower Boat Launch. ETA is five minutes." "Roger 419. The LT is awaiting your arrival." Sam and Tom looked at each other and knew there would be hell to pay.

When Sam pulled into the launch's parking lot a uniformed police officer waved him over to a safe parking area that could accommodate his truck and the attached trailer with the Jonboat. It seemed that the situation had drawn not only curious citizens but also, the Newspapers, Fire Department personnel, police cruisers that were in the area, and ambulances. The large and usually only half used parking lot was nearly full. Lieutenant Gene Alban (badge number 402) stood near the boat ramp as the wardens winched the crippled Carolina onto her trailer. Other people just milled about the boat ramp and parking lot, took pictures of the damaged patrol boat or just gawked at the situation. The game wardens were silent. They continued to get the Carolina secured and clear of the busy boat ramp.

Alban had walked over to the middle of the parking area and raised his right arm into the air turning his outstretched hand in a counterclockwise direction. The signal was noticed at once by more than just the wardens as everyone had their eye on the distraught lieutenant. One or two at a time, the wardens reluctantly meandered over to where Alban waited. Once all attending Fish and Game personnel were accounted for, Alban looked at the group of officers that had formed a semi-circle in front of him. There was a quiet minute or two when nothing was said, then Alban started in his usual stern and even toned, lecture mode which rose as did the color of his face. "Are you guys for real? You actually pushed the victim's boat over the dam and the knocked them into the falls. I can't believe what I'm hearing." The berating and chastising continued and got worse with every sentence. The wardens stared at the ground while Alban had his way with them. Sam kept his eyes fixed on the lieutenant. *Yeah. You said it, LT. What you … heard. You weren't out there.*

Disgusted with Albans behavior, Sam looked away from the group and over to the beached Searay the Hover Craft had towed in. It lay on the beach near the boat ramp, broken and half full of water. The little boy who had been an occupant and part of the whole scenario sat on the Searay's bow and continued to cry. His soaked and disheveled parents stood in front of him helpless, not knowing what to say to the little lad. Sam turned from the group of wardens and headed for the family right in the middle of Alban's speech. "Moody … Where do you think you're going?" Sam kept walking toward the beached Searay and ignored the lieutenant. "Moody, don't you turn your back to me. I asked you a question." Sam had now tuned Alban out and was focusing on the little boy sitting on the Searay's bow.

The parents watched Sam approach and stepped to the side as it was obvious Sam wanted to speak to the boy. He walked up to the Searay and pulled himself up onto the bow and sat next to the boy. The youngster looked up at Sam for a moment and Sam asked, "Do you remember me?" The boy nodded that he did and looked back down at the sand still sobbing. Sam paused a moment then offered, "I'm Corporal Moody. That was me in the green boat. It was pretty scary out there wasn't it?" The little boy just shook his head in an affirmative manner but continued to stare into the sand. Sam paused a moment and stared into the sand with the boy, then asked, "Can you do me a favor?" The boy looked up at Sam with a confused look on his face and nodded. "When you go home for lunch and you're sitting there with your mom and dad, I'd like you to tell them everything you remember about what just happened out there." The boy just continued to stare Sam in the eyes. "Everything … just as you remember it. Can you do that for me?" The boy nodded again and Sam shook his hand. "Okay, pal - thanks, I'll see you later."

Sam eased himself off the Searay's bow and started back toward the gaggle of wardens still standing in the middle of the parking lot. The boy's father stopped Sam, "Thank you officer. We know what you just did. That was wonderful. We will have that discussion." Sam nodded his head and the boy's mother reached over and hugged Sam, "Thank you for taking that special interest in our boy." "You're welcome, Ma'am. Talk about the whole thing … every detail. Let him get it all out." The distressed and embarrassed couple smiled and nodded their heads. Sam turned and continued his walk back to where Alban and the remaining wardens waited.

"Moody!" Alban had been watching Sam as he approached the downtrodden group. "I want to see you over by the Jonboat." Sam walked by the group of wardens and waited for Alban to meet him. It was out of earshot from the rest of the crowd. "Corporal Moody, if you ever turn your back on me like that again, I will have those stripes." Sam had been looking at the ground and expecting the worst. When Alban finished he looked up and right into the lieutenant's eyes, "How dare you?" Alban's jaw dropped and the corners of his mouth went wide as if he didn't understand. Sam didn't give him a chance to speak, "If you ever talk to me or the rest of those guys like that again, I'll give you the stripes." Alban couldn't believe what he was hearing. Sam continued, "Those guys just risked their lives to save a family in trouble … in very dangerous river conditions I might add … and the rest of the guys came back to the river on their day off to see if they could help from shore … and you have the balls to ream them out in front of their peer departments … not to mention the general public and the newspaper people?" Alban opened his mouth to speak but Sam cut him off, "Yeah, the rescue was flawed. It happens, but that is not what these guys wanted. They were here to help and they did their best." Sam just stared at the embarrassed lieutenant. Alban knew Sam was right and for once had nothing to say. When Sam realized Alban was not going to speak, he turned away and went to his truck. Alban just watched him leave.

★ ★ ★ ★

Chapter 13

Once again, Monday morning arrived with the usual animosity about what may happen at morning roll call. Sam tried to keep a clear head and not surmise about what Alban might say about the flawed rescue attempt of Sunday morning. The roll call room was full, everyone in attendance, and quiet for once. Everyone kept to themselves and went over notes or fiddled with their uniforms but the room was quiet.

Lieutenant Alban walked in and everyone stood. "Sit," was his response. The lieutenant stood behind his podium and looked through his notes. After a few minutes he looked up and into the room of officers. "Does anyone have a question or comment about yesterday's river recovery on the dam?" The room remained silent. Alban panned the room and looked at each officer. "Nothing?" The room remained quiet. Alban looked back down at his papers on the podium. "Okay, routine patrols today. Stay alert … Be safe. Dismissed."

Alban turned and left the room. Everyone looked at each other in utter amazement. The usual thirty minute roll call meeting had lasted all of three minutes. At first everyone just sat in their seats as if they had done something wrong. Then one by one they got up from their chairs and went to the cruiser bays. Some just shrugged their shoulders and welcomed the opportunity and headed for the cafeteria to get a coffee before shift.

Sam was the last one out of the room and as he turned to head for the cafeteria he heard his name from down the hallway. "Corporal Moody." Sam turned around to see Alban standing by his office door. "May I have a word please?" Sam walked up to the waiting lieutenant and stopped in front of him, "Sir?" Alban motioned with his head for Sam to go into his office.

Sam walked up to his favorite place in front of the lieutenant's desk. Alban closed the door, walked past Sam and sat down at his desk. Alban looked Sam square in the eye for a moment then said, "This is not about the recovery. This is about your discussion with me in the parking lot yesterday afternoon." Alban's face was dead pan serious. Sam kept his eyes locked on the lieutenant and said nothing. Alban paused a moment, "I was out of line yesterday in how I handled the recovery's outcome." Alban paused again then continued, "I wasn't out there. I wasn't seeing it for what it was–and you were. I reacted to the radio transmissions and what the other support groups were suggesting. As Unit Commander, it was the wrong thing to do, especially in front of them and the general public." Sam continued to stare forward with no emotion. Alban continued, "It took some balls to do what you did - walking away from me while I was chewing out the whole lot of you ..." Alban stopped and waited for Sam to say something but Sam remained silent. Alban continued, "I know that's not your style and after thinking about it, I felt you must have thought you had a good reason. The parents of the boy on that boat came up to me and told me what you did for him. That was good work, Sam. No one else even thought about that kid once he was ashore." Alban stood from his desk, "I guess everyone needs to be brought down a peg once in a while." Sam stood and shook the lieutenant's hand. "Is there anything you'd like to add, Sam?" Sam thought a moment, "Everyone has their days, Sir, but as long as I'm in here there is something I'd like to speak to you about.

★ ★ ★ ★

CHAPTER 14

"What is it that you wanted to speak to me about, Sam? Have a seat and tell me what's on your mind." Sam sat in one of the guest chairs in front of the lieutenant's desk. "Well LT, It's been a couple of years now and we still haven't a clue as to who was responsible for Officer Hanks' murder, and we still don't know what happened to those other guys that were with him in the Checkmate." Alban sat back in his chair, "Go on, I'm listening." Moody continued, "I'd like to investigate the incident. I made a promise to Hanks when I came home from the academy." Alban raised his eyebrows but said nothing. He continued to stare at Sam. "It was after graduation. I stopped by the cemetery on the way home and visited Hanks' grave. I told him we'd do him right."

Alban continued to watch Sam. After a long minute Alban asked, "Do you realize what taking on an investigation means … especially a murder investigation?" Sam nodded his head in a way to indicate that he did. Alban paused again, knowing the officer part of Sam had no experience in this area yet. "Sam, this kind of work is more dangerous than your regular patrols. You are putting yourself in danger's way when you don't need to." Alban paused for effect, "It also means long hours away from your family. It means digging back into old homicide files, looking through mug shots, interviews, increased patrols on the river, especially at night … all extra time when you could otherwise be home with your kids." Sam was sitting bolt upright in his chair and began to relax a bit. He was beginning to feel a little more at ease since he had finally presented Alban with the news that he wanted to do the investigation. "Doesn't matter LT … I made a promise."

Alban sat up in his easy chair, picked up a pencil and began tapping it on his desk as if he was thinking out loud. Sam looked determined. Finally, Alban broke the silence, "Okay, Sam you got it. You're the lead on the case but you must keep me informed every step of the way … and no hero stuff." Sam broke from his stiff pose in the chair, "Thank you, LT. May I pick my partner or will you be assigning someone to me?" Alban narrowed his eyes as he watched Sam, "Who did you have in mind, Sam?" Quickly, Sam put in, "I'd like to have Tom Stafford with me and Pat James when you can spare him. After all, it was the three of us out there that night." Alban looked down at his desk then back at Sam, "You can have Stafford. You'll have to request James when you need him for special ops … if it comes to that. I can't afford to have three officers on one investigation." Sam thanked the lieutenant again, stood from his chair, and started for the door.

Alban spoke as he watched Sam leave, "Sam." Sam turned to face the lieutenant. "Remember. Keep me informed of everything you find and everything you plan to do." Sam was matter of fact, "Yes sir, I will." Alban nodded, "Okay, Be safe," and waved Sam off as to dismiss him from the office.

★ ★ ★ ★

CHAPTER 15

The stage was set. After Alban had agreed to let Sam conduct the Hanks investigation, Sam and Tom Stafford made plans to start their night patrols on May 30, the night before Memorial Day. Traditionally, Memorial Day weekend brought out all the antsy sailors that had been excitedly awaiting the good boating weather ... as well as the would be sailors who needed guidance and practice. Most of the boating violations that happened on the river had to do with Memorial Day weekend or as everyone knew it ... the beginning of summer.

The sun was setting on the Connecticut River. It was approximately 8 PM and it was a clear night. The fast and ferocious waters of April had subsided and the river level was almost back to normal. There was an orange hue that struggled to retain its fading color as the sun began its decent behind the West Hills. The bottom of high flying cumulus clouds reflected the last rays back down into the quiet river valley almost as if to say good night. The water moved in a calm but steady flow and with the darkening corridor, appeared as a black sheet on the water. A slight but warm breeze was present but almost unnoticeable.

Tom Stafford and Sam Moody walked along the newly constructed town dock to the waiting Carolina Skiff, Marine One. The boat sat in its slip looking like new. Extensive repairs had been made to her after the last ordeal on the Thompson Dam and also a few additions were implemented. The two marine patrol officers wore what the bad guys referred to as 'goon suits.' The Class C uniforms consisted of a short, light jacket that ended just above the officer's hip. Under the jacket was a brown button down shirt with a sewn on badge over the left breast. Because it was still cool at night, a black turtleneck shirt was worn under the button down shirt and sported the initials TF&G in gold on the left side of the turtleneck collar. Dark blue jeans covered the lower extremities with black jungle boots for the feet. Each officer wore his issue combat belt with keepers that attached to a regular waist belt to support the .357 magnum revolver that rode just under the officer's right arm in a high rider holster. The high rider was designed to position the revolver high over the officer's hip and generally kept it from snagging equipment on the boat. Situated between the holster and the belt buckle were two speed loaders that also hung from the combat belt, loaded with six silver jacketed .357 magnum hollow points in each. On the opposite side of the holster a Maglite was positioned with a folding hunter knife just behind that. A brown baseball cap topped off the entire outfit with a Fish and Game logo over the hat's bill.

Both Tom and Sam had their issue PFD's slung over their shoulders as they walked to the boat and were required to wear them no matter what the weather or temperature conditions. Another law enforcement badge hung from an outside loop on the left side of the PFD so citizens could make an easy distinction in a confused situation.

Sam was the boat's skipper so he jumped into the Carolina, got behind the helm and opened the radio box where all the electronics were. While Sam busied himself with the boat's electronics system, Tom began checking equipment and getting lines ready to free the Carolina from her slip on the dock.

It was almost dark and Sam looked up at the waiting Tom Stafford who stood on the dock, bowline in hand. Sam turned on the running lights and nodded to Stafford, "Okay, Tom – all set. Hop in." Tom pushed the bow of the Carolina away from the dock and into the waiting current while throwing the bowline onto the deck of the boat. He took a step back and jumped into the Carolina's already freed stern as it came by him on the dock. Sam had already started the ignition and kept it in neutral until he felt the current start to grab, then he eased the throttle forward leaving the Carolina's resting place in as quiet a manner as possible.

Sam drove the Carolina out into the river and began angling her toward the channel. Tom knew the drill and moved to a position next to Sam and behind the helm's windscreen to operate the search light. Sam spoke without taking his eye off the bow, "Remember to turn that off once we get by the old piers. Anybody upriver will be able to see that for miles. It's moon bright tonight so we'll use that to keep us in the channel. Move up to the bow to watch for any debris coming at us that I can't see from here." Tom turned to look at Sam with a smirk, "Yeah, okay Skipper." Sam just smiled as he watched the river slide under the bow in front of them.

Navigation past the old piers and into the channel was uneventful. Progress was slow but once the Carolina cleared the ledge area Sam dropped the prop back down to normal cruise depth and increased RPMs. The water was like glass and the boat seemed to skim the surface. Still, Sam kept the throttle at half full FORWARD. There was no need to attract attention with speed or sound … especially tonight. The silhouette of the patrol boat would be invisible from a distance and unless Sam turned on the light bar over his head, the entire outline of the boat, including the Bimini top over the skipper's head, would be undetectable.

Tom had been sitting in the bow ever since they left the ledge area and had chosen the night vision binoculars to watch the shoreline. Sam kept the boat as smooth as possible so Tom could look for discrepancies on shore as well as on the water. The Carolina continued to slide up river quiet and smooth … just another water craft moving upstream.

Minutes passed, then Tom raised his fist into the air so Sam could see it, and opened his hand. Sam throttled back and slowed the boat to one third FORWARD and turned off the running lights. Voices travel easily over large expanses of water so Tom spoke quietly. "I have the marina in sight … Speed Dreamers … I can see the sign over the boat house." With that, Sam angled the Carolina closer to shore in an attempt to snuggle into one of the many little islets that dotted the area in front of the marina.

There was a perfect little cove in one of the islets that couldn't be seen from the marina itself but provided a view of anyone coming out into the main body of the river. Sam pulled the boat up in front of it and throttled back to REVERSE, wiggling the Carolina into a tight fit with the branches of willow trees hanging over her Bimini top and scrub brush scratching along her starboard and port sides. Tom smiled, "Go ahead, scratch her up and give Alban another reason to invite us to his office." "Kiss my ass, Tom. This is a perfect vantage point. The boat is just one of the tools of the trade … don't give a shit about scratches right now."

Dan Hayden

Minutes turned to hours. The mosquitoes had started but weren't in force yet … just enough to make it mildly uncomfortable. Finally there was movement on the dock. Two people came out of the bar next to the boathouse and were preparing to get one of the docked boats ready to go out on the river. Tom flattened his body against the Carolina's raised bow deck and continued to watch through the night vision binoculars. Quietly he said to Sam who had been watching the river with his own binoculars, "Looks like their coming out … silhouette looks like a lowrider too. They're going to be passing right in front of us." The engine start was loud. The driver revved it a few times making a huge disturbance in the quiet little lagoon of moments before. "Okay, second guy is in the boat." Sam put down his binoculars and got behind the helm. "Here they come." The driver of the lowrider must have slammed his throttle all the way forward and came speeding out of the marina full bore, passing in front of the Carolina by less than fifty feet, showing her port side. The lowrider's occupants were looking straight ahead and never noticed the patrol boat sitting in its tangle of willow trees and scrub brush.

Tom braced himself and held onto the bow rail, "Get ready for the wake." The aftermath of the lowrider's pass developed a huge wake that tossed the Carolina from bow to stern in the willow trees. "Shit," Tom was holding his cheek. "Tom, you okay?" "Damn willow branch got me across the face. I'm okay."

Sam stayed behind the helm. "Are we going after them or what," Tom was ready for the chase. "Nope. We're going to wait right here and see what happens when they come back." Tom was shocked, "They just blasted out of that marina at top speed. They broke the law right there." "Tom, we're not here for that. We have to watch the goings on around here

100

to see who is doing what and when, so we can find Hanks' killer. We're going to have to watch some more of that stuff until it's time to act. Patience, Thomas." Tom stared at Sam a moment and nodded his head.

★ ★ ★ ★

CHAPTER 16

The Carolina remained in her islet hideaway gently rocking in the waves from a quiet river. The two marine officers patiently sat in the shadows and awaited the return of the lowrider to the Speed Dreamers marina. Tom Stafford sat in the boat's deck chair forward of the helm with his night vision binoculars glued to the river scene off his port side. Sam sat on the captain's bench seat watching the marina and neighboring bar, Joey's Speed Trap, situated next door. Now and then one of the officers would quietly squash a mosquito or brush an insect away. Slapping or swatting would make too much noise.

"Hey, Sam," Tom was speaking just above a whisper. "I can hear an engine in the distance. Can't see them yet but it's definitely getting louder." Sam sat farther back in the boat surrounded by heavy brush and willow trees. Sounds weren't as easy to hear as they were from Tom's position where the entire bow was open to the main body of water. Sam whispered back, "They must be coming back. It's got to be them at this hour of night. I haven't seen any other boat traffic since they blew out of here an hour ago."

The night breeze had picked up a little and was more steady than intermittent and it was definitely darker. The high cumulus clouds had dropped lower and stacked up, closing off the moon light. Sam continued to listen for the approaching boat with his eyes still on the marina and bar. "Yeah, I hear it now. Sounds like it's coming from upriver." No one said a word. The only other sounds were of the insects that continually tried to land on their human hosts and the new breeze blowing through the willow branches. As the breeze picked up, the long loose willow branches swept the top of the Carolina like a broom.

The lowrider seemed to be heading right for the hidden Carolina. She approached from upstream and was angling in toward the several islets that dotted the area in front of the marina. Tom watched the approach, "At least they have their running lights on. Hope they don't turn on any searchlights or beacons … they're coming right for us." Tom flattened his body against the raised deck of the Carolina's bow and Sam crouched behind the helm. The lowrider came in hot, almost as fast as it had when it left. The lowrider blew by closer than it had before, this time making a port turn toward the marina, showing the Carolina her starboard side. The resultant wake was worse than before as the lowrider came to within thirty feet of the Carolina's bow.

Willow branches pounded the Carolina's Bimini top and the scrub trees that encroached on her hull on three sides scraped and scratched the patrol boat as it rode the wake. Tom kept his head down and muttered, "Damn! It's almost as if they know we're here and are giving us the business."

Sam watched the low-rider as it approached the water in front of the slip area. "If he doesn't throttle back soon, he's going to slam into that dock." As if on que, the driver throttled all the way back to neutral, and rode the stern wake into his slip. There was a loud, dull crack as it contacted the dock and deflected into the adjacent boat parked next to it. "Tom murmured, "There's another violation … reckless operation in the second degree." Shaking his head Stafford whispered, "These guys are something."

Sam was watching the bar next door. "Shhh … we've got four guys stumbling out of the bar. They're coming toward the dock." The people that had just exited the bar came outside and stood under the bar's sign, Joey's Speed Trap, and were canvasing the area around the parked boats. They were talking to one another but the conversation was not discernable. Suddenly one of them pointed in the direction of the Carolina. The party of four broke into a run heading for the dock area. From his flattened position on the bow's deck Tom warned Sam, "Uh oh. Looks like they spotted us. One of them is pointing at us and now they're running for the dock." Sam quieted Tom, "Stay put. I think they're pointing at the two guys in the lowrider that just slammed into the dock." As luck would have it, the lowrider was positioned directly between the men outside the bar and the Carolina.

The four men from the bar descended on the two occupants in the now dormant lowrider. An aggravated and loud altercation ensued that escalated into a pushing and shoving match. The lowrider's passenger fell off the dock and into the black water. Several expletives stood out from the confrontation but general conversation was too far away to be understandable. The lowrider's driver still stood in the boat and reacted to his passenger's fall. He ran from the open bow area to where the helm is, reached down and picked up something long and black. He climbed out of the boat and onto the dock holding the weapon in a batter up position as he approached the group of four.

Tom spoke first, "Is that a bat? Could we be that lucky?" Baseball bats aren't usually standard equipment aboard any boat and Tom was alluding to the idea that maybe they had stumbled onto the right people early in the investigation. Sam continued to watch as the scene unfolded. The driver walked up to the angry group and began taunting them with the butt of the long weapon. He thrust it at one man hitting him in the stomach, and did the same as another man got to close. Tom and Sam turned to look at each other. Sam raised his eyebrows as if to say 'what are we watching?'

Tom zeroed in on the man's weapon adjusting the fine focus for the night vision. "Looks like a baseball bat to me. He sure is handling it as if it is." The group began to break up. The most visibly shaken man was still speaking but pointing to the boat parked next to the lowrider. Tom looked over at Sam, "That guy must be the owner of the docked boat the lowrider hit when they slammed into the dock. I think they heard the crash from inside the bar and came out to see what happened … and his buddies came out with him." Sam was still watching the group of angry men begin to disperse. "I agree. The fact that a baseball bat was inadvertently used as a weapon is coincidence or is what that guy keeps in the boat for surly situations is a good lead. We're going to have to go ashore when they leave to search that lowrider." Tom rolled his eyes. *Here we go.*

★ ★ ★ ★

CHAPTER 17

There were several cat calls, threats, and hand gestures that followed as the angry group of men dissipated. Finally the dock area was quiet and abandoned. Screeching tires and the sound of car engines fading into the night could be heard in the distance, however the partying inside Joey's Speed Trap seemed to continue undaunted.

"I think they're gone," Tom Stafford was still watching the dock area. "Maybe." Sam added, "Let's wait a bit longer … just to be safe." After a few minutes Sam asked, "Where is that two man raft?" Tom motioned to a couple of access doors built into the deck side below the bow's raised deck that closed off the Carolina's hold area, "I have it stored in the bow's hold." "Okay, wait a couple of more minutes and get it out while I get the Carolina secured. I want to paddle straight across the lagoon and up to the dockside where that guy fell in. Looks like there's a ladder there and the view will be obscured from the bar."

After a few minutes, Tom retrieved the raft and used the onboard hand pump to inflate it. Ready for the water, Tom let the raft slide over the bow's end and into the lagoon. One by one they lowered themselves over the Carolina's bow and into the two man raft. Sam dropped into the raft first, then Tom. Each man unhooked a paddle that was fastened to each side of the raft and pushed away from the Carolina.

"Nice, discreet strokes Tom. We're not in a race. I'll follow your strokes with mine since I'm in the back. Let's just get there without anyone noticing. If we get caught out in the middle of this lagoon, we're dead meat."

The two officers paddled steady and slow with the slightest of water sounds. Once they reached the ladder by the dock, Sam tied off the raft while Tom climbed the ladder to the dock above. Reaching the first level, which was a walk around to the parked boats, Tom stayed in a low crouch so his silhouette couldn't be seen against the river background. He scanned the area and motioned to Sam, "It's clear. C'mon up." Tom and Sam stayed in a crouch and ambled over to the now tied up lowrider. Tom looked the boat over, bow to stern, "That's a Checkmate class boat for sure. Look at those sleek lines!" Sam had been looking over the other boats docked nearby, "These are all high performance boats. There's even a three-point racer sitting in that cable hoist over there." Tom looked around the quiet marina, "No outboards, no sailboats, no small craft. This place is a playground and these are the toys."

Sam motioned to Tom in a horizontal fashion with his head, "Okay, keep watch. I'm going to board the lowrider." The lowrider's gunnels were about one foot below the dock. The first thing Sam did was check for the bat. He looked behind the driver's deck chair and saw a long black object lying between the chair and the hull. Sam pulled a handkerchief from his pocket and grabbed the would-be weapon. Raising it over his head he whispered to Tom who watched the area above, "It's a bat alright. I'm going to take a picture of it and put it back. Don't know if it's thee bat, but it's possible."

Tom crawled over behind the transom and looked down for the boat's name, "Can't quite make it out but it's not Streaker." Sam looked up, "Well they said it wasn't their boat that night. See if you can get the bow numbers. A cursory glance of the rest of the boat showed nothing. Sam climbed back up onto the dock and crouched next toTom. "Okay, we got enough for tonight. Let's get out of here. Don't want to overstay our welcome."

In the darkness the two men made their way over to the dock's ladder and back into their raft. Paddling across the lagoon seemed like it would take forever but soon the Carolina's bow appeared in the darkness from under a mess of low hanging willow branches.

Sam and Tom climbed aboard the Carolina and prepared for departure. The trick was to get the Carolina out of the tight parking space without snapping too many tree branches, if any at all. The braking of the willow branches would make too much noise and attract undue attention to the whole mission. Sam turned on the ignition, while Stafford watched the dock area. Then slowly and gently, Sam eased the throttle forward at dead slow speed. There was some scratching and squeaking along the sides of the hull but nothing that could be heard from across the lagoon.

As soon as the Carolina was clear of its jungle garage, Sam turned the helm hard over to port bringing the Carolina over to the river side of the islet and out of site of the marina. He brought the engine to idle and let the vegetation covered patrol boat drift downstream. When they were well out of ear shot, Sam engaged the throttle to half ahead full FORWARD and headed for home. It had been a productive night.

★ ★ ★ ★

CHAPTER 18

"You gotta' go back." Lieutenant Alban Sat in his office across the desk from Sam. He had just read Sam's report and listened to Sam's entire accounting of last night's patrol. Alban paused while Sam's jaw dropped. "You've got to lift some finger prints off that bat." Sam started to say something but Alban cut him off. "This is a murder investigation, Sam. We can't take anything for granted." The lieutenant looked back down at Sam's report, "You say here in this report that it's not the same boat we rafted up to two years ago." He looked up at Sam, "How do you know that? Did you check the registration?" Sam answered quickly, "No sir. It was a Checkmate but it wasn't the same color, and we really couldn't see the name on the stern because of the angle we were at." Alban sat back in his chair and threw his pencil onto the desk as if he was giving up. "Sam, the boat was probably re-painted, the name changed, etc., etc., anything to camouflage it … especially if it was involved in an attack on anyone. The one thing they can't change is the HIN (Hull Identification Number). It's on a metal stamp permanently attached to the transom on the starboard side and sometimes riveted to the inside of the engine compartment. Since it's out of the way and out of sight, the location is usually forgotten. If you get that info we can compare that to its registration and who it's registered to."

Sam looked like he was at a loss for words. "Well it was pitch black out there, LT. We lost the moonlight when the skies clouded up and I couldn't use my Maglite for fear of being seen. We were in plain view of the bar, Joey's Speed Trap." Alban just nodded his head. "Next time, be more discreet with the Maglite keeping the beam in a downward direction … less obvious."

Sam said nothing but now felt as though he hadn't really accomplished anything on that night patrol. *Damn, I didn't even plan on going ashore last night. I just took the opportunity after things escalated. Can't say that to the LT. He'll think it's just another excuse.*

Alban broke the silence, "Sam, You guys did okay last night. You took some chances, picked up some info, got some leads, and most of all didn't get noticed. You still have a lot to learn. You will always have more to learn. I know that you know that stuff about disguising the boat and changing hull numbers. That's Marine Patrol 101, academy stuff. You've got to be thinking that way on the scene … when it counts. Now you have to go back and do it all over again. Take the same risks for you and your partner, all over again. As for the driver … he may be the guy … maybe not. You only have the mental picture in your mind from two years ago. That would never stand up in court." Alban paused and looked down at the report again, "We need those prints so I am requesting the Police Department assign an officer to you." Sam became defensive. *Oh man, now he's assigning cops to us. Doesn't think we can handle it. Damn it.*

Alban continued, "I have requested Officer John Grey. He is trained in dusting for finger prints and other crime scene procedures." He'll also be back up for you and Stafford."

Sam nodded his head looking a little forlorned. Alban knew the meeting was at an end and let Sam know it was time to leave. "Okay, good discussion. Get with Stafford and make a plan. Outline it. Anticipate everything. Discuss it. Then come back and tell me what you're going to do." Sam got the message and stood from his chair. Alban looked back down at the report and waved Sam off with a flip of his hand. "Have a good day.

★ ★ ★ ★

CHAPTER 19

Sam spent the rest of the day thinking about how unprepared and unthinking he had looked in front of the lieutenant. He had hoped for the opportunity to avenge Hanks' death and finally got permission from Alban, and come up short in front of the one person he needed to impress. *What's he thinking now? I go in there with that damn patrol report thinking I had done something so great only to find out I missed just about everything. Ahh, he's probably laughing at that little show I just put on in there.* The biggest insult was that the lieutenant felt it was necessary to call the Police Department for assistance.

Sam struggled with the same thoughts for the rest of the morning. Finally it was lunch time so he left the marine division office and headed for the PD's cafeteria in the next building. Sam felt like being alone so he could sort things out before he talked to Tom Stafford. *A quiet lunch by myself in the Cafe. I have to get a handle on this before I talk to Stafford ... get myself into a different frame of mind.*

Sam pushed open the double doors to the cafeteria to see Sergeant Mike Smalls sitting at the first table facing the entrance. Immediately, Smalls hailed Sam, "Hey, Moody. Come on over ... got some news for ya." Sam stopped dead in his tracks. Marine Corporal Sawyer was also present and sat adjacent to Smalls. *Aw shit. He probably talked to Alban and now I'm going to spend the next hour getting my ass busted by these two.*

Sam slowly walked over to the table. Smalls actually looked happy to see him. "Come on, have a seat." Smalls moved his crutches and pulled out a chair from under the table as Sam approached. Sam was a little apprehensive. Sergeant Smalls was usually kind of ornery and not so hospitable. Sam sat down and prepared for the worst. Smalls began, "I wanted my marine officers to be the first to know. I am retiring from the Unit. As of July first, I become citizen Mike Smalls … regular guy." Sam drew a sigh of relief. He knew Smalls must be joking because everyone knew Smalls was way too young to be retiring. Sam cracked a smile, "Yeah okay, Sarge … and I'm Santa Clause." Smalls laughed, "No really. It's an early retirement. Medical discharge. My knee is so fucked up I can't be trusted in dangerous situations anymore. According to the doc, it can go out at any time." Sam watched the animated Smalls. *He can't be happy about this … especially if they alluded to the fact he's now medically incompetent.* Sawyer added, "Its true Sammy. We finally got rid of him."

Smalls continued with a bigger grin than was appropriate, "Yeah, that night rescue in April, below the dam really screwed my leg. They said I'm relegated to office work at reduced pay or early retirement, so you know what I chose." Sam realized Smalls and Sawyer were telling the truth. "Sarge, are you okay with this?" Smalls shrugged his shoulders, "Gotta' be … right? Life goes on, man. I got a lot of other things I want to do anyhow." Smalls sat back in his chair, "Yup, no more nights of getting called out of bed to talk a jumper off the Thompson Bridge, no body recoveries … no more shit from you guys. It's going to be great."

★ ★ ★ ★

CHAPTER 20

Sam sat in his usual place at the dinner table. Peg was busy talking with the boys, Matt, Steven and Joey. Everyone was talking and laughing about the day's events. Sam, however, was quiet and stared at his plate, pushing vegetables around with his fork. "Sam, what's the matter? You haven't said a word all though supper," Peg displayed a frown that was half smiling and half serious. Sam looked up from his plate, "Huh? Oh sorry. Just thinking about my meeting with Alban this morning. He thinks he has to call in the cops to help Stafford and me." Peg's expression turned into a frown. She glanced at the three boys who looked confused, "Okay you guys, you're done. Bring your dishes to the sink and go do your homework. I have to talk to Dad about something." Grasping the opportunity to be dismissed, the three Moody boys got up and obeyed their mother. When they had left the room, she leaned across the table from where she sat, "Okay, big boy … What's going on?"

Sam shook his head in disgust, "I need a break. Need a diversion." Peg gave Sam that no sympathy look she was famous for, "Oh, the great Sam Moody doesn't need help? He can do everything." She paused and her voice got a little higher and more sarcastic. "Are you kidding me, Sam? You had a class in taking finger prints ... no actual experience. That's what cops do. Game wardens bring in the bad guys and let the cops take the mug shots, fingerprints ... all that office stuff." Sam continued to stare at his plate. Peg continued, "Just do your job. You can't afford any mistakes, this is for your buddy Steve Hanks. You want good information if you want to get those guys so let the people trained for the part do it ... no matter what their title is."

Sam slowly nodded his head, "Yeah, I know, but there was so much Alban called me on this morning. Maybe if the meeting had gone better I wouldn't be feeling like this." Sam got up and collected their dinner plates. "This is your first homicide investigation, Sam. It's going to be a learning experience. It's also almost two years old. It's not going to be easy." She came back to the table and sat down again. "Why don't you call Cyrus and go fishing? He'll take your mind off things." Sam nodded his head, "Yeah, that sounds like a good idea. I'm off tomorrow afternoon. Maybe we can steal away for a couple of hours."

★ ★ ★ ★

Sam and Cyrus were on their way to the town's boat launch, sometimes referred to as the 'upper boat launch.' The sign for the town's local bait shop, Yankee Bait and Tackle, appeared as Sam rounded the corner onto North Main Street in the old section of Thompson, just east of the old train station. Cyrus piped up, "Hey let's stop in at the bait shop for a minute. I want to see if Guy has got any of those plastic black worms. A friend of mine said the smalleys (small mouth bass) are going nuts over them." Sam agreed and pulled over in front of the local bait shop.

The brothers walked into the quaint little shop located about a block from the boat launch. Cyrus knew Guy carried the worms but also knew Sam would enjoy visiting the store owner. Guy was the typical weathered and experienced fisherman. He always had a story to tell and always asked what you were fishing for. The talk would be another distraction for his brother. Guy looked up from the glass case he always stood behind, "Well," Guy bellowed. "What did I do to deserve this honor ... two Moodys at the same time?" Sam took the opportunity and started talking to Guy about fishing on the river while Cyrus left them alone and busied himself with a fly fishing display across the shop.

True to form, Guy asked where on the river they were headed and Sam told him they were looking for smalleys tonight, up near the Massachusetts border. Guy's eyes lit up, "Hmm ...,up by the border. Heard about a guy catching carp up there the other day. Fishin' out of a Checkmate to beat all." Cyrus heard Guy's statement and turned to look at the two men. Sam raised his eyebrows, "Using a Checkmate for a fishing boat isn't against the law ... a little unorthodox maybe ..." Guy leaned across the glass case, "Yeah, well that's not what's weird about it. I heard every time he brought one in, he slammed it with a bat or something long and skinny. Then he'd throw it overboard and do it all over again. Can't understand why he just didn't let 'em go."

Cyrus stopped looking at the flys and walked over to Guy and Sam, "Hey, Sam you gonna' talk all afternoon or are we going fishing? Smalleys should be hitting in about an hour." Guy just rubbed his bearded chin and smiled. Sam frowned at Cyrus, "You're the one who wanted to stop in here. Now you're in a hurry." Sam shook Guy's hand, "See ya, Guy. I'll be in next week to check those shop permits. Once a year thing ... it's time again." Guy raised his hand to his head in a kind of a half salute, "Good fishin' fellas." Sam and Cyrus left the shop.

The two Moodys launched Sam's canoe at the town ramp upriver of the Thompson Dam and paddled toward the Massachusetts line. Sam had to promise no 'shop talk' for Cyrus to agree to go on the fishing trip so there was no conversation about the man fishing in the Checkmate. It was hard for Sam at first, especially after what Guy had just told him. He just filed that info into his memory and resolved not to talk to Cyrus about it.

Cyrus and Sam were approaching their favorite fishing spot. It was north of the old piers on the west side of the river, about a half mile from the state line. A glacial boulder that rested on the bank marked the location. Cyrus was in the front of the canoe, "This is the place. I'm going to throw the anchor." Sam stopped paddling as Cyrus took up the anchor line to make it taut and secured it to the canoe's forward thwart.

As the two fishermen set up their tackle, Sam looked up in time to see a motor boat pulling a skier. There was only the driver and the skier, no spotter to watch the skier which Connecticut State Law required. "Cyrus pull the anchor. That driver is pulling a skier with no spotter." Cyrus looked up quickly at the passing boat and skier, then back at Sam. "No, Sam. You are not on duty … remember? We're out here to relax so you can put all that stuff aside for a while." Sam just looked at Cyrus a moment realizing he was right but said nothing. Cyrus continued, " … besides, how do think we're going to catch them in this canoe?" Sam sheepishly replied, "We'll follow them. They're probably headed for the peninsula on the State Line." Cyrus shook his head negatively, "Forget about it. Get to fishin.'

★ ★ ★ ★

Chapter 21

(first week of June)

The week was passing slowly. Wednesday night's fishing excursion with Cyrus was frustrating at first but had helped Sam to depressurize a little. He sat at his desk in the marine division office thinking about what his plans should be for the next step in the Hanks investigation. *I have to come up with something soon. The one thing I don't want is for Alban to ask me what it is and not have an answer.* Sam continued to ponder the situation as he stared out the window across from his desk. In his peripheral vision he noticed a book about U. S. Navy Seals that Sawyer had been reading in his spare time. Sam picked it up and began leafing through it. Suddenly it was lunch time and Sam was engrossed in the book.

One of the areas Sam had stumbled on was how the elite force of soldiers found the suspect they were after. They entered the suspected area of activity a person of interest might have a reason to visit and watched for the person that didn't fit in. It could be the way he looked, walked, dressed or talked. The plain and simple actions of the POI (person of interest) would almost always expose his credibility as the sought after suspect. *Hmmm*, Sam thought. *Maybe it's time for Tom Stafford and me to pay Joey's Speed Trap a visit ... but as patrons this time. I'm going to want Pat James in on this one. We'll go in there to have a beer in our civvies and just watch ... maybe ask a few questions if we get engaged in conversation with the locals.* Sam felt good. He had a plan. *Got to get the boys together and discuss details.*

The rest of the day passed without incident and Sam's mood had lifted appreciably. He had a plan. It was only the beginning, but it was a good beginning. The drive home was good and for once Sam began to feel confident about the investigation.

Sam jumped out of his truck, walked across the gravel drive to the farmer's porch and ran up the steps. Peg Saw him coming and met him at the door. Before she could react, he planted a big kiss on her lips and continued into the cabin. "Wow! What has gotten into you?" "Get the boys, we're going out for dinner tonight." "Sam, I already started dinner. That's a nice thought but it's the middle of the week and the boys have homework. Maybe this weekend ... Okay?" Sam turned around, still smiling, "Oh, okay, Honey. That's fine." In an instant he was gone to change into his jeans and sneakers. Peg watched him go. *These mood swings have got to stop. I'm going to have to find out what caused the sudden mood change this time.*

Dinner was more active than usual and Sam was more a part of it than usual. Tonight Peg was the quiet one as she watched Sam talk and joke with the kids. Finally, it was time for dishes and homework. "Okay you guys, get to the books. I got the dishes tonight." Peg piped up, "Okay buddy, what's this all about?" Sam was clearing the table as Peg watched, "Nothing really. I got an idea today that is going to help the investigation and I know Alban is going to like it. I finally have something to work with and it just feels like a large weight has been lifted off of me." Peg got up from her chair, nodded to herself and began putting dishes away. "Okay, thanks for the help but I'll finish up here. Why don't you go relax in your chair for a while?"

Sam sat in his easy chair in front of the dormant fireplace and began to drift off. Peg rushed in, "Sam! Dispatch is on the phone." Sam glanced at the clock and picked up the phone by his chair. It was 8 PM. "Moody here." "Sam, this is Thompson Dispatch. Get the boat. Suicide at the upper boat launch. Witnesses report a car just drove into the water. Sunk with all inside. State Police Divers will be assisting ... toning them next." Sam stood from his chair, "On my way."

★ ★ ★ ★

CHAPTER 22

(first week of June)

It was a beautiful sunset and the sun was falling below the West Hills. Sam was almost to the boathouse. He picked up his portable radio and keyed the mic, "419 responding. ETA to boathouse is five minutes." Dispatch came back quickly, "419 – Dispatch. Proceed directly to the boat ramp, 410 and 429 have the boat. Await your arrival for launch." "Roger Dispatch, 419 out." Sam made the turn for the ramp. *How did Sawyer and Beech get there before me?*

Sam pulled into the first open space in the lower parking lot and screeched to a halt. Police cruisers, ambulances and fire trucks littered the launching area. Sam jumped out of his truck, opened his truck box and pulled out his issue PFD. Turning, and in a half run, he saw the Carolina sitting on her trailer, lines detached and ready to slide into the dark river. He began thinking about the response time. Dispatch had the clock running even as he ran for the boat. *Too bad we couldn't keep the boat tied to the dock 24/7. It would cut response times in a big way.* Although the Carolina had a new dock, river conditions didn't allow for the patrol boat to be docked there permanently. It was brought back to the boathouse for routine maintenance periodically and if weather conditions were questionable.

In a dead run, Sam reached the waiting Carolina, jumped up onto one of the trailer's fenders and hopped over the starboard gunnel. Sawyer stood on the ramp holding the Carolina's bowline and Frank Beech sat in Car 6 ready to back Sam and the patrol boat into the river. Sam reached up over the helm and opened the radio box to retrieve the Carolina's ignition key and turned on the electronics making all the gauges and dials come to life. Then he flipped the switch for her running lights. When Beech saw the lights come on he started backing the Carolina down the ramp. Sam was almost done with everything except for the ignition. The engine couldn't be turned on until at least part of the engine drive cowling was submerged.

The Carolina started to slide off the trailer and into the river. Sam braced himself and held onto the helm and one of the stanchions while watching the Carolina's stern. The moment the stern hit the water, Sam radioed Dispatch to stop the clock, "419 – Headquarters. Marine One is wet." "Roger 419, good luck." Sam started the engine.

When Frank saw the Carolina was clear of the trailer, he pulled the trailer out of the water and parked it and Car 6 across the parking lot. Meanwhile John Sawyer tossed the bowline into the boat and walked to the side of the ramp where Sam would pull in to pick up his crew. Sam turned the key and choked the engine. The Carolina's 40 horse Honda came to life. Still moving backward into the river, Sam nudged the throttle to NEUTRAL until the engine settled out and then to FORWARD. Frank and John grabbed hold of the Carolina as it slid up onto the beach and entered from opposite sides. Sam reversed the throttle and yelled over the noise, "PFDs." As the crew donned their gear, the Carolina backed out and into the river's current.

The fire department's captain ran out to where the Carolina was departing from and hailed Sam. Waving his hands in an X pattern over his head, he yelled to Sam. "Yo, the boat. Come on back," and pointed at the beach as if that was where he wanted Sam to park. Frank was standing next to Sam, "What in hell does he want? Hell of a time to ask for a boat ride." Sam moved the throttle back to FORWARD and eased the boat back up onto the beach. The captain came up alongside the Carolina's starboard bow, "Hey Skipper, do you mind if me and my diver ride with you?" Sam looked at his own crew and knew what they were thinking. He looked back down at the short and stout looking captain with disgust. *It's all about credit. Wants his boy to dive on the car when we snag it so the fire department will make the headlines. Just using us as their horse again.*

The Carolina was seventeen feet in length and pretty spacious under normal conditions. She could accommodate two more people but no more. "Sure. Come aboard but you guys will have to ride up front. My guys are going to be dragging hooks (anchors) on either side in the back so we'll need the room to move around." The captain nodded at his diver and then climbed in himself. Sam backed the Carolina out into the river again to begin his search for the sunken car.

The Carolina was the lead search vessel and Dispatch began assigning grid patterns as usual. Everyone knew it was no longer a rescue, but a recovery, since the driver had meant to do what she did. Still, the car and body, or bodies had to be brought back up. "419 from Dispatch. You are lead. Start your pattern along the east shoreline one hundred yards south of the ramp and end one hundred yards north.

Pattern is north and south out as far as the first pier from the east shoreline." Sam grabbed the radio mic hanging from the radio box above his head, "419, Roger. East shoreline. Starting pattern." One by one the search boats from surrounding towns entered the river and were assigned their associated patterns. Sam turned the boat downstream and made the turn for an upriver pass. As they approached the ramp area, Sam turned to Frank and John, "Drag the hooks starboard and port - fifty feet of line." Frank Beech and John Sawyer threw their anchors out behind the Carolina as she continued her search line parallel to the shore. Sam kept the speed just fast enough to keep way on against the oncoming current. The Carolina and her crew settled into a back and forth pattern parallel to the shoreline for the better part of an hour. "Guys, on our next pass up river, let a little more line out and I'll slow a little in front of the ramp." As soon as Sam finished talking he turned back to face the bow and got a face full of wooden oar. "Son of a bitch!" Sam yelled into the night. One of the firemen up front had grabbed an oar and pushed it through the space between the helm's windshield and the electronics console under the Bimini top. Sam was immediately blinded by the blunt end of the oar and had instinctively put his hand over his face. "Sammy, you okay?" Frank grabbed Sam by the left shoulder. "Want me to take the helm?" Sam didn't answer but shoved the throttle back to NEUTRAL. He rubbed his eyes with the back of his left hand, "I can see ... a little blurry, but it's coming back." He set his jaw and looked to the two firemen moving about in the bow of the boat. His temper flared but he picked his words carefully, "Captain, there is no need for you and your diver to be handling any boat equipment. When we snag the vehicle you can do your thing. Until then, please just sit and be patient." The diver complied and sat on the raised bow. The captain just glared at Sam, stood to the side, and held onto the deck railing.

It was getting windier as the night grew older and the temperature began to drop. Sam looked at his crew. They looked cold and showed signs of shivering. Frank and John would never complain or ask for a break. "I'm taking her in so everyone can warm up. Pull the hooks in." Frank and John complied and Sam turned the helm over and started for the beach. The captain stood in front of the helm's windscreen and thrust a forefinger into Sam's face. "Where do you think you're going, mister?" "Looks like the crew is getting cold. I'm taking her in so people can get a coffee and warm up." The captain snarled back at Sam, "I am the ranking officer on board this boat … Corporal, and I'm telling you to turn back and stay out here." He pointed out over the dark horizon at the other three boats busily performing their patterns. "No one else is going in so we aren't either."

Sam continued on his heading for the beach, "Captain, I am the Skipper of this boat and I am responsible for the safety of this boat as well as her crew. I am taking her in." As Sam completed the sentence, he goosed the engine a bit and beached the Carolina. The captain walked over to the helm and got into Sam's face. "You're in a lot of trouble now boy. I'll just have a talk with your lieutenant about what you did." Sam looked over the Carolina's bow and saw Alban pacing the beach. "That's him right over there, sir." "Wise ass, we'll see if you ever drive again." With that, the disgruntled captain walked up the beach for a discussion with Alban.

Sam began shutting down the Carolina as he watched the captain speak to Alban. John and Frank stood next to Sam as he nodded to the Red Cross trailer, "Go ahead guys. Go get some coffee. See you in fifteen minutes." John jumped over the Carolina's port side and onto the sand below. Frank remained at Sam's side, "I'm stayin' with you, Skipper. If that blowhard comes back here with Alban, I'm gonna' give 'em a piece of my mind." Sam shook his head from side to side, "Nah, I'm good. Go get a coffee and get me one too, will you?" Frank eyed Sam a moment, nodded his head, and followed John to the Red Cross mobile station.

★ ★ ★ ★

"Is that what he did," Lieutenant Alban kept a serious look on his face while hiding the slightest hint of a smile. His left arm was crossed over his chest and supported his right elbow. The lieutenant thoughtfully rubbed his chin with the fingers of his right hand. "Yeah, that's what he did alright. A corporal telling a captain how it's going to be … I want that guy busted." Alban continued to look down at the illuminated beach sand, "Let me get this straight. You were a guest in his boat." The captain nodded in an affirmative way. Alban continued, " …and he's the skipper of that boat?" The captain again nodded. Alban looked up from the sand and into the captain's eyes, "He's the skipper … He is the boss no matter how many stripes or bars you have sewn onto that hat of yours. If you don't like what he says … don't go in his boat." Alban let his gaze sink into the man for a long moment then walked away from the surprised captain.

Sam could hear little of the conversation from behind the helm of the beached Carolina but knew what Alban's answer was from the tone of what he did hear and the facial expressions that had been exchanged between the two officers. Sam smiled to himself as he busied himself checking the fuel and battery gauges. John and Frank appeared at the Carolina's starboard side ready to board again. Frank was holding two coffees. "At your service, oh mighty Skipper. Coffee is served," and handed Sam his hot black coffee.

Once everyone was back aboard Sam nudged the throttle to REVERSE and powered the flat bottomed Carolina off the beach. "Everything okay, Sam? I see that captain stayed ashore." Frank looked concerned. "Yeah," Sam smiled. "Guess he doesn't want to ride in our boat anymore."

★ ★ ★ ★

CHAPTER 23

(first week of June)

The Carolina continued her assigned search pattern as directed by Dispatch. Another hour passed. Suddenly the hook on Frank's side grabbed hard. Even though Sam had the boat at minimum speed, the grab made the whole boat lurch to the port side. Sam quickly shoved the throttle back to NEUTRAL. "Think we got something, Skipper." Frank pulled on the anchor to make it taut. "Give it a couple of good, hard pulls, Frank." Frank did so and the hook held. Sam looked over at Sawyer, "John, shine that searchlight around where the anchor line meets the water." Frank piped up, "Got an oil slick over here with bubbles rising from around the anchor line."

Sam signaled the police divers who were suiting up on shore. "Marine One to State Dive. We have snagged a hard object. Suggest you come out and have a look." "Marine One, Roger." Sam looked over at Frank, "Tie a buoy around that anchor line. We're going to be here a while."

The anchored Carolina sat dormant in the cold, black water. The crew stood at their stations quietly observing the area and periodically showed the searchlight on the buoy that marked the supposed target. Sam kept his control display lit so the depth sounder could continue to give bottom readings.

"Here they come." Frank reported as the State Dive Team left the beach in their rubber Zodiac. The state dive boat seemed to be outfitted with the latest in every contraption associated with marine rescue and recovery. The Zodiac pulled up to the Carolina and rafted up along her starboard side. "Where's the buoy, Skipper?" "Stern – port side," Sam gestured with his left hand in the general direction. With that, the Zodiac's skipper nodded to the first diver and he rolled head first into the river, olive roll style. "Divers Two and Three stand by."

Minutes passed as everyone on board the Carolina and Zodiac watched the water and the bubbles that rose from the diver's scuba tank. Finally, the diver surfaced right next to Sam's position in the Carolina. The diver spit out his mouth piece, "There are two cars down there. One is on top of the other." Sam looked down at the diver in the water, "What color is the car on top?" "It's a white sedan of some sort." Sam turned to look at Frank and John, "That is what was reported by witnesses." Sam turned to the diver, "Did you see anyone in the car?" The diver shook his head in a negative way. "Check again and around the wreck. She could have floated free … and see if you can get a flashlight on the license plate." The diver nodded his head in affirmance and followed the buoy line back down. Sam looked over at the dive boat's skipper who waved to him. "It's okay Fish and Game, you are Command, we will follow your lead." Also, Dispatch had already penned the Carolina as lead over the air. Sam acknowledged the dive boat skipper with a loose salute and nodded.

The night moved on slowly and it seemed to be getting colder. Divers Two and Three had both taken their turns at the bottom of the river, and now the last diver surfaced and crawled aboard the anchored Zodiac. The dive boat's skipper motioned to Sam after a short meeting with his divers. The Carolina and Zodiac were literally lashed together so all the two skippers had to do was lean over each other's gunnels to talk. "No need for you guys to stay tied up to that buoy line. We're going to be in and out of the water all night. We'll replace your anchor line with ours and re-attach your buoy to it. You guys can head in. We've got it from here."

Sam nodded, "Okay sounds good. Find anything yet?" "Nope. No body yet … its real dark down there with a lot of silt. The car it's sitting on top of is ancient and looks like it's been down there a long time." Sam shrugged, "Okay thanks," and started the Carolina's motor. *Seems like they're holding back a little about what they're seeing down there. They've been swimming around down there for two hours and they still can't give me any information except that it's a white car on top of another car that's been there for a while.* Sam shook his head and felt a little disgusted. "Okay boys, we're heading in. Go get comfortable in your trucks. We have to stay on station until they find the body. Call your wives once we get in and beach the Carolina."

Once the Carolina was secured and Frank and John had gone to their trucks, Sam called Peg from the beached patrol boat. He stared out at the midnight sky as his home phone rang. The breeze was steady and cool as it moved his hair around the sides of his marine patrol hat. When the last of the search boats had been pulled from the water, the river had become a quiet place again. Sam watched the outline of the West Hills on the opposite shore. The moon had reappeared from behind the clouds and shone across the dark river like a white carpet that became wider as it got closer.

Finally Peg answered, "Hello, Sam?" "Yeah, it's me. Looks like I have to stay out here all night … at least until they find the driver's body. You okay?" There was an uncomfortable pause but Sam let it play out. "Why can't they let you come home for some sleep? There are other guys in the Marine Division." Sam replied in as soothing a tone as he could muster, "It's the rules, Honey. I'm going to crawl into the bed of my truck … got a sleeping bag in there. As long as someone brings me coffee in the morning, I'll be okay." Peg looked into the phone and felt skeptical, "Well, be careful," and hung up the phone. *It seems like I'm saying that more and more lately.*

★ ★ ★ ★

CHAPTER 24

(first week of June)

Morning arrived on the Connecticut River to find the Carolina and three patrol boats from neighboring towns beached on the sand. The parking lot was quiet except for the snoring of several marine patrol officers who lay sleeping in different trucks and police cruisers. It was sunny with a slight breeze and the night's chill still lingered soon to be melted away by the days shining. The boats had been parked in the dark and appeared as if they had washed up on the beach during an angry storm. Boat trailers were lined up across the boat launch and had been neatly positioned to utilize the least amount of available parking space.

Someone's alarm broke the silence of the quiet and peaceful boat launch. There were groans and audible yawns, mixed in with associated expletives that described what it might feel like to spend the night in the bed of a truck or the backseat of a police cruiser. "Let's go – State Dive Team – On the beach. Red Cross will have your coffee and eggs out soon. Gear up." The dive boat's skipper walked around to all the vehicles lightly tapping on windows and car hoods.

Sam was lying face down in the bed of his truck with his head resting on the tailgate. "Shit. What a terrible night." His muscles ached all over from the hard truck bed and the cool air that had made sleep almost impossible. Sam rolled out of his sleeping bag and swung his legs over the side of the tailgate. He stood, stretched, and started to round up his own crew.

Red Cross began passing coffee around and everyone grabbed a quick breakfast. The state divers were out on the river thirty minutes later and had tied up to the buoy that marked the location of the sunken car. The dive boat skipper walked up to Sam. "We think we have a body. It's definitely the right car. Can you get the fire department to winch it out of the water?" Sam looked at the skipper. *What do you mean-you think you have a body?* Sam nodded his head and called Dispatch, "419 – Headquarters." "Good morning, 419. What is your pleasure?" Requesting one of the fire trucks with winching capabilities. We're ready to pull the sunken car from the river." "Roger, 419. It's on the way."

Dispatch sent a large hook and ladder to the accident scene. The truck parked at the back of the boat launch to give the car room when they pulled it from the water. Two divers took the hook and cable from the winch and walked out into the water where the dive boat captain brought it out to the buoy. Diver Number One took the winch hook down to secure it to the submerged white car. Sam's crew stood on the beach and watched the scene with the other boat crews. A crowd of onlookers gathered at the top of the upper parking lot where a policeman held them. No one said a word.

The diver surfaced and swam over to the zodiac. When the dive boat skipper signaled, the fire truck started winching the car from the river. The cable strained and made metallic noises as the winch collected more and more cable. Soon the back end of a white car could be seen coming up from the shallows. The color was dull at first and became brighter as it neared the surface. The car's trunk came out of the water, then the roof broke the surface. The rear quarter panels were now showing above the waterline and then everyone gasped. The driver had apparently been trying to save herself as the upper part of her body was out of the rolled down window with her hands and arms frozen in a reach for the sky fashion. She still had her seat belt on and rigamortis had already set in. The winching continued and the body was brought in with the car. Police at the upper part of the parking lot held up large tarpaulins in front of the crowd of onlookers to protect the victim's privacy.

Sam watched the scenario unfold and wondered about all the secrecy from the night before. Sam's radio crackled to life, "419 from Dispatch. You and your crew are cleared from the boat launch. Thank you and go get some sleep." "419 - Roger." Sam looked over at his motley looking crew, "Okay guys. Pack her up and dock her at her berth over there. We are out of here."

★ ★ ★ ★

CHAPTER 25

(first week of June)

Sam was on the phone and sat at his usual spot in the marine division office, sitting across from Sawyer, as he listened to Lieutenant Alban recount the final details of the sunken car recovery. "So, everything considered … it was determined to be a suicide. The victim had just been released from a mental health facility that morning." Alban's tone was monotone as he described the details of the case. "It has been confirmed by witnesses interrogated on scene that she was alone when she drove into the river and started to panic as the water began entering the car." Alban paused for a moment, "Any questions, Sam?" "No sir. I'll get my skipper's report in by noon time today." Alban's tone was easier now and not so business-like. "Sam, I am addressing you on this one because you were the skipper on scene that night … you realize that?" Sam said he understood and Alban continued, "I am moving Corporal Frank Beech over to marine and promoting him to Marine Corporal-First Responder." Sam smiled and said nothing. Alban went on, "We need a marine sergeant to fill in for Sergeant Smalls' position. His last day is this Friday. Do you have any suggestions?" Sam let the hint of a smile show at the ends of his mouth, "How about Corporal Sawyer? He has been Marine Corporal, second to Smalls, for some time now. He's a good man." Alban answered with, "Yes, he is a good man ... and good at what he does, but he isn't one to take responsibility for the boat under extreme conditions. He also hates paperwork and I need to rely on the marine sergeant to keep good files." Alban paused for what felt to be an extremely long time. Sam let the awkwardness of the quiet phone build. He wasn't about to let Alban put him in a compromising position. Finally, Alban continued, "I was thinking Tom Stafford would be a good fit."

Sam was elated to hear Alban was going forward with Tom Stafford's career and was considering him for such a responsible position in the Fish and Game Department. What confused Sam was why Alban was running any of this by him. "Well Sir, if you're asking my opinion, I think Stafford is a great choice. He would be skipping the corporal rank but in my eyes, he has all the necessary skills and personality traits the position requires." Alban nodded his head, "I considered the fact that he'd be skipping corporal, but had he not gotten into that trouble last November, he would be a corporal right now. He has paid his dues and he has all the same marine training that you do ... except for the patrol boat captain certification. Captain Fletcher and I feel you could train him for that." Sam replied immediately, "Of course–absolutely." Alban paused and his voice became softer and his tone more direct, "He would be your boss, Sam."

Sam was taken aback a little. He had not pictured Stafford's promotion in the way Alban had just described it. He was all for Tom Stafford and wanted the very best for him but didn't like the way the lieutenant put it. "It's not about rank, sir. Tom is the man for the job and I'll do whatever it takes to help him get there. We work well together and know each other very well too, so I think it will be a good fit." Alban finished the phone call by saying, "I'm glad to hear you say that Sam. We will advise Stafford by the end of the week. Have a good day."

Sam hung up the phone slowly. He didn't like feeling this way especially about his good buddy Tom Stafford. *Am I that wrapped up in myself and my career that I haven't considered anyone else's … especially one of my best friends? It's just that I have always been the take charge guy.* That was when Sam realized he was taking Stafford's promotion all wrong. *Like I said, it's not about the rank or how many stripes you have on your shirt. We do this job for a reason, most of it for the concern and safety of others. What matters is how well we do it and how good we are at it.*

Sam immediately felt better about himself. He had almost let the administration and their micro managing techniques influence the way he considered his reason for being on the Unit in the first place. Sam rose from his chair and went for a walk to clear his head.

★ ★ ★ ★

CHAPTER 26

(June)

It was a long ride home from the PD. Sam was happy for his pal Tom Stafford but couldn't get by the feeling that he had been overlooked by the Thompson law enforcement administration because of the New Hampshire incident. How long was he going to have keep paying for that? He knew it was a place he alone had put himself in and should accept that fact. Hell, he was lucky to still have a job, especially the one that he had always dreamed of.

Soon Sam's gravel drive appeared up on the left. He pulled in and parked in his usual spot in front of the barn. It was a few minutes before he opened the truck door. *I have to put on a face for the family. Can't let them think I'm feeling sorry for myself especially because one of my best friends is going to be promoted over me.* Sam got out of the truck and walked over to his farmer's porch, climbed the stairs and stood in front of the cabin's entryway. *Okay, here goes.* Sam walked in and gave his usual greeting to the family. Peg was at the kitchen counter preparing dinner and the kids were in the TV room watching the tube. He walked into the bedroom and changed into his civvies. Peg called out, "Dinner is ready, everyone. Come and eat."

There was the usual banter at the Moody table with Peg intervening to keep things under control. Sam tried to add to some of the conversation but fell short every time. Finally, dinner was at an end and Peg dismissed the children from the table and looked at Sam, "Okay, what's up? Bad day?" Sam glanced up at her knowing she was hard to keep anything from. He just kind of smirked and nodded his head. " … May as well tell me now. You know I'll get it out of you sooner or later."

Sam still tried to avoid the subject. Peg began to search for something to get Sam talking. *Hmmm, maybe he's heard something about Farmer.* "Have you heard the latest about Jake Farmer?" Sam looked up from the table with a questioning look. Peg continued, "It appears he had another heart attack in the rehab he's been in … happened about a month ago." Sam still showed no emotion. "It was a mild one but it's going to mean another month there before they can transfer him to the state prison where he can start doing his time."

Sam knew Peg really wanted to know what was on his mind so he explained the phone call with Alban earlier in the day and how he felt glad for Stafford but sorry for himself at the same time. He was confused that he could feel both ways. "I think Alban is playing with your head, Sam. If that phone call went as you said it did, he is still trying to make you pay for what you did in New Hampshire … and to pick one of your closest colleagues over you is kind of obvious." Sam felt a surge of anger at the thought, "Shit! He busted me two ranks, suspended me, and reduced my pay … not to mention the cold shoulder treatment I get whenever he's around. You'd think that would be enough." Peg smiled and looked down at the table, "It's never going to be enough, Sam. You were his most promising officer. In his eyes you let him down ... so he's going to take it out on you ... probably for a long time to come. You still have your job ... be thankful."

Sam and Peg sat awhile at the table not saying anything, then Peg stood up, "I have to get the boys lunches ready for tomorrow. Why don't you give your old fireman buddy a call? Take him fishing or hiking. You never call him anymore. It'll be a nice change for you." Sam looked up from the table, "You mean Larry?" "Yeah, the fire chief from the next town over ... what was it ... Mansville?"

Sam rolled his eyes, "No, it was Manville and he was Deputy Chief, not Chief." "Yeah, whatever. Call him. You guys used to have so much fun together. I have never seen anyone that could make you laugh like that." Sam thought for a moment and nodded his head, "Maybe I will."

The next day Sam drove to work thinking about Larry Spencer. He wondered how they could have let so much time get between them ... one of his best friends. It had been about three years since he'd seen the man. Shows what family and job obligations can do to relationships. Sam decided to call Larry today at lunch time.

★ ★ ★ ★

It was 1205 hours, or as laymen would say 12:05 noon. Sam picked up his office phone and called the Manville Fire Station, "Thompson Fish and Game, here. May I speak to the Deputy please?" "Yeah, sure. Who's calling please?" Sam smiled. The old, mischievous feeling had come back with a simple phone call, "Tell him it's the Mayor and I'm not happy." The phone was silent for several seconds, then

Larry's familiar voice came through the phone, "Yes sir. This is Deputy Chief Spencer. How can I help you?" Sam's smile got wider and more wicked, "Did they tell you I'm not happy, Deputy?" There was a slight pause then Spencer replied, "Moody, you are such an asshole. You don't call me, you don't write for what … three years … and then you call me at work pretending to be the Mayor?" Moody smiled, "Hey, up yours too, pal. Good to hear your voice."

The two old friends talked for a bit then Sam cut to the chase, "Look, Lar. I need some fun time. Things are getting a little serious around here. I need some of that Larry and Sam bullshit … you know the stuff that just seemed to happen when we got together?" Larry came back quick, "Yeah, I know what you mean. The stuff you make happen, usually at my expense." Sam laughed, "I don't know what you mean by that Deputy, but yeah, that stuff."

★ ★ ★ ★

Chapter 27

(June)

The weekend had finally arrived. It was Saturday and Sam and his old friend Larry had agreed to go fishing in the afternoon. Sam promised to take him to all the best fishing spots. Sam poured himself a cup of coffee and walked out to his usual place on the porch. He took a sip of the hot coffee and placed the mug on the railing. What a great idea Peg had. Sam had felt differently all week anticipating an afternoon of fishing with one of his oldest and best friends. It was a fun relationship. Nothing was ever serious when they got together and nothing was ever really as it appeared either.

It was 1:00 in the afternoon and Sam pulled into the upper boat launch with his canoe tied to the bed of his truck. He planned on arriving a little before Larry so he could have the canoe ready and in the water before Larry arrived.

Sam pulled his truck up to the sandy beach next to the boat ramp. He glanced over at the Carolina sitting quietly in her slip. *Not today lady. Today is all about fun.* He turned back to the task at hand – unload the canoe and get the fishing gear stowed.

The canoe with all of its gear was finally ready. Lifejackets were placed in the canoe's bow and stern. Since it was after Memorial Day, it was not required to wear them but only to have enough for each individual in the canoe. It crossed Sam's mind to place a child size under Larry's seat in the bow just to get the fun started but he decided not to push the short man thing just now. Sam stood back and looked at the canoe. It was a pretty emerald green made by Bear Creek, a company in Limerick, Maine. Both lifejackets were present, one under each seat. Fishing poles, tackle box, paddles, anchor and line – all there. Now all that was missing was Larry.

Sam gazed out at the calmly flowing river. It was a beautiful day with a slight breeze. There was however, a moderate amount of boat traffic. Sam's daydreaming was interrupted, "Hey partner! You didn't leave anything for me to do. I would have helped you get this thing in the water." Sam smiled back at Larry, "Don't worry pal. You're going to do most of the paddling." Larry put his hands on his hips, "Oh, I see. I have to sit in the front again." Sam said, "It's not the front, it's the bow … and if you would learn how to steer and control a canoe I'd let you sit in the stern, but until that happens … "Larry cut him off, "Go to hell, Moody. I'm as good as you are." Sam smiled. It was time for the short man comments. "If I'm in the bow I'm not sure you could see over my head. You need to be able to see in front of the craft to steer correctly." Larry just stared at Sam for a moment, "Still the same, aren't ya?" Sam just smiled back at his old friend. "Let's get to it old buddy."

Larry Spencer had been one of Sam's closest friends through the years. Before the academy they had seen each other routinely especially for some of the kid's events like camping trips and family vacations, but as the family got older and Sam's job changed, the two men as well as their families began to drift apart. Larry was quite a bit shorter than Sam and a lot thinner. Sam liked to say he had chicken legs and chicken arms. He sported a mustache and had short crew cut style hair now beginning to grey. When the two men were together they fit the 'Mutt and Jeff' stereotype to a tee. One of their favorite things was to goof on each other, no matter what the occasion. In the end, Sam would always sum up the experience by letting everyone know it was always Larry's fault.

Sam slid the canoe into the water and motioned for Larry to step in first. Larry looked at Sam and kicked off his sandals. He stood by the side of the canoe in what appeared to be a new green bathing suit … probably purchased just for the occasion. "What in hell are you wearing Spence (Sam's nickname for Larry)?" Sam tried to appear shocked. The bathing suit was of the old military style, or 'trunks' as they were called, with short baggy legs and an elastic waistband for the waist. "This is my new swim suit. The wife picked it up for me," Larry was obviously happy with his new swimming attire. Sam smiled viciously at Larry, "Oh, okay. I thought it was part of your fire … man issue stuff." "Go to hell, Moody. I'm done talking to you for a while. Start paddling." "Okay, Captain," Sam replied half laughing as he pushed the canoe off the beach.

The two canoeists paddled their way up river against a moderate current. Larry sat in the bow with his back to Sam and paddled a decent rhythm as Sam had told him his position in the canoe was akin to the engine room on a motorized vessel. There were specific expletives from the bow but it was all in good fun. Eventually, the conversation they had at the launch was forgotten and they settled into their routine discussions about fishing and boats, water clarity, and what the families were up to. Sam, however, had not forgotten about the ugly swim suit Larry was wearing.

"Okay Lar, let's start fishing here. Stop paddling and we'll just drift and cast as we slide down river." Sam had angled the canoe to the west side of the river just north of where the Hanks tragedy took place. The peninsula on the Massachusetts line was visible and to the north approximately one mile. "Aren't we going to drop anchor," Larry had turned to look at Sam. "Nah. We'll just fish and drift for a while. The current here isn't too bad and it'll carry us over some of the best smallmouth bass sites." Larry turned back around, stowed his paddle, and busied himself with preparing his fish pole with a lure.

Once Larry had turned back to the bow of the canoe, Sam stealthily raised his fish pole over Larry's head and let his lure drop toward an opening between Larry's waistband and the small of his back in an attempt to snag Larry's swim suit. The plan was to grab the elastic band with the lure and start hauling it upward so he could announce he had a big one on the line. Unfortunately, the timing was bad and Larry turned quickly to his left to address Sam. The lure caught hold of the waistband and got Larry's attention. "What the hell, Moody! You hooked my new suit." Sam began laughing, "Okay, okay, stop moving around and I'll reach across the canoe and unhook it." Larry had turned back to face forward while Sam got on his knees in the stern and reached across the length of the canoe in an attempt to unhook the snagged lure. "If this doesn't beat all. You are really somethin' Moody. We haven't even got our lines wet and we have a situation on our hands." Sam was now stretched out along the length of the canoe. His knees were on the floor of the canoe in front of his seat and his chest and belly rested on the two thwarts that gave the canoe its rigidity. In this position, Sam was barely able to reach the lure. As he dipped his two fingers down inside the waistband, Larry surmised another trick and spun wildly to his right driving the lure's treble hook deep into Sam's forefinger. "Oww," Sam yelled from his outstretched kneeling position. "Now you've done it. The treble is in past the barb. Don't move anymore … Every time you move the hook goes in farther." Larry had to remain seated, facing front, so he couldn't even turn toward Sam to complain. "Oh, so now it's all my fault. You hook my suit and it's my fault the hook is in your finger."

Larry began to notice people on the river bank pointing at them as well as a few boaters smiling as they passed by. Since neither man could paddle due to the awkward circumstance, the river's current began to take over. The anchor had not been thrown so the canoe began to turn end for end as it drifted lazily down river.

More complaints from the bow, "We're a laughing stock. The Town of Manville's Deputy Fire Chief and a Thompson Marine Patrol Officer. Connecticut's finest - shit! Oh God, I hope no one has recognized us." Sam couldn't keep from laughing although the pain in his finger was getting worse. Fingers bleed easily and the wound looked much worse than it was. Sam still couldn't move or he risked sending the hook further into his finger. From the side, it appeared as if Sam was kneeling in the stern of the canoe while reaching across the top of the canoe with his right arm outstretched toward Larry's backside and his hand on the back of Larry's swim suit.

The two old friends continued to drift downriver at a lazy pace, the canoe turning end for end as no one was in control. "Sam, I can hear the falls. We've got to fix this now. If you don't do something soon, we're going over the falls with your hand on my ass." Sam was staring straight down at the bottom of the canoe. "Spence, you need to calm down so I can think. Worst comes to worst I'll just rip the sonuvabitch out of my finger." Larry turned his head a little as if to look back and over his shoulder at Sam. The look and tone seemed to be that of sarcasm, "Oh, don't do that. There has to be a better way."

Sam craned his head to the right so he could look over the starboard side. The canoe was making slow turns in a counter clockwise fashion as it drifted with the current. He waited for the canoe to come around so he could look downriver. The Thompson Bridge was approaching and the dam was about two hundred yards downriver from that. He looked over his other shoulder and saw they had already passed the old stone piers. *How did we ever miss those?*

The Thompson Dam was a low head dam and had caused some terrible accidents this spring alone. The dam was an old design and was dangerous because it was invisible to an approaching boater from upstream. The top of the dam was at river level and spilled water over to a secondary surface level four feet below. Sam brought his head back to center and calmly spoke to Larry in a serious tone. "Lar, you're going to have to take your swim suit off." Larry objected loudly, "Are you nuts? I'm not doing that – too many people around."

Sam let the thought sink in another minute then said, "Lar, stand up slowly and drop your swim suit. Do it slow and I'll raise my hand with your ass as you stand up. When you get your balance slowly drop the suit to your ankles, then step out of it … one leg and then the other." Larry didn't respond for a couple of minutes. The canoe was quiet for the first time all afternoon. Then Larry broke the silence, "Moody you are such an asshole."

Larry did as Sam instructed. Once Larry was free of the suit, Sam grabbed it, collected himself, and inched back to the stern of the boat, swimsuit in hand. Sam looked up and realized Larry was still standing there in his most natural position. "Larry, sit down. People are going to talk." "Fuck you, Moody. I'm never coming on one of these adventures of yours again." Sam unhooked the suit from the lure and tossed it back to his embarrassed partner.

Sam wrapped his finger with some duct tape he had found in the tackle box and began paddling the canoe back up stream. No one said a word all the back to the boat launch.

Finally, Sam beached the canoe and hopped out onto wet sand. Larry remained in the canoe still fuming. Sam gave Larry a playful slap on the shoulder as he walked by him. Once at the truck, Sam opened his cooler and pulled out a cold beer. Larry watched Sam and decided to join him. Sam took a long pull on his can of beer while Larry watched with a long look. "Where's mine?" Sam smiled back at his old friend, "You have to apologize first."

★ ★ ★ ★

Chapter 28

(June)

The fishing trip with Larry, although eventful, was successful in bringing back the old Sam. No fish were caught and fishing lines never saw the water but it was needed time spent with one of his oldest and best friends. The atmosphere was back to mischievousness and good natured tom foolery. It had been a much needed break for Sam. Larry had soon dismissed the awkwardness of the afternoon to just another of his and Sam's unforgettable afternoons ... one they could reminisce about as they sat in their rocking chairs during the twilight years.

Sam drove to work thinking about the escapades of the weekend and smiled. It was funny now but it had been little more than a consideration at the time. It was a great new day and Sam went back to enjoying the beautiful scenery as it passed outside his truck one more time. Of course there would be many more of the same but to Sam it was always a new experience.

Roll call was routine and Alban had announced Tom Stafford's promotion to marine sergeant. The usual clapping and slapping on the back followed with cat calls and the like. Sam and Pat remained at the back of the room and let their buddy soak it all in. They were happy for him.

As the last of the wardens left the roll call room Tom turned and approached Sam and Pat who were still seated in the rear of the room. "Hey Sam, I need a word with you, if you don't mind." Pat stood up, "I didn't want to talk to you either … Sarge," and proceeded to leave the room. Tom turned to Pat, "Hey, wait a minute." Pat turned around with a big grin, "Just kidding. Nature is calling and that is more important than talking to you. Congratulations … Sarge." Pat left the room.

Sam was still seated in his usual place and waited for Tom to begin. Tom leaned against a desk in front of Sam and started, "Sam, this doesn't change anything between us. I didn't even apply for the position." Sam smiled back, "Yes it does. You're the boss now. They needed a replacement for Smalls and you are a good fit. I told Alban that." Tom was at a loss for words so he just stared at the floor. Sam asked, "Do you still want to continue as my partner on the Hanks investigation?" "Of course," replied Tom. "You're still in charge – it's your investigation. Besides, you still have to teach me some of that covert stuff and all the marine patrol procedures." Sam smiled and nodded in approval. "Alban has assigned one of the cops to us … a John Grey, because of his experience with taking fingerprints and so on. He let me know in one of my last meetings with him that we weren't up to speed on that end and because of that we have to go back to the Speed Dreamer's marina to dust the boat for prints. Still don't know if that Checkmate we climbed into that night was the boat involved." Stafford nodded his head in agreement as he thoughtfully stared at the floor.

★ ★ ★ ★

Sam sat at his desk in the marine division office and picked up the phone. Dispatch came on the line," Thompson Dispatch. Can I help you?" "Good afternoon ... Moody here. Can you connect me with Officer John Grey please?" "Oh, Hi Sam. He's on shift right now ... due to be back in the station at 5:00 PM. I'll give him a message to give you a call when he gets a chance." "Okay. I'm off at five too. If we don't connect I'll try to find him before he leaves the P.D." Dispatch hung up.

Sam busied himself at his desk and went over his plans again for the next sortie to the Speed Dreamers marina. He pulled out his file which had grown in size to two inches thick and also a customer list of past and current patrons that kept their boats at the marina, the class of boats docked there, associated boat names, and registration and hull identification numbers. The marina's list also required the boat's color and 'descriptors' which was radio slang for a concise but accurate description of the boat, which included stripes, two tone coloring, make and model, etc.

The desk phone rang, "Marine Division ... Moody here." The voice in the phone was familiar but not one Sam recognized readily. "Hi Sam. This is John Grey. Dispatch called and said you need a word?" Sam smiled, "Yeah, John. Lieutenant Alban appointed you to help us dust some prints at a marina up river regarding the Hanks murder of two years ago. How do you feel about that?" John's reply was immediate, "Oh, yeah. The rookie game warden that was killed on his first patrol ... right? I'm excited. It's a chance to get out of the cruiser and do something a little different. What are we doing?" Sam was doodling on a pad as he spoke to the policeman, "We need to go back up to the marina under the cover of darkness and check out a boat that we believe may have been involved in the Hanks' murder. We've got some info on the boat and what's in it

but we need some prints. Alban says you are the expert."
John nodded with a smile, "I'll do what I can." Sam replied,
"Okay, good. Warden and Marine Sergeant Tom Stafford
will be working with us. He has accompanied me on the
past two sorties up there and wants to stay a part of it. I'd like
to have a briefing with you and Tom tomorrow morning for
a visit up there tomorrow night." Officer Grey was eager,
"Sounds good, Sam. I'll arrange my schedule. My Captain
told me to do whatever it takes. I guess I'm on loan to you
guys for however long you need me." "Okay, John. See you
in the morning after roll call. We'll meet in the cafeteria."
Sam hung up.

★ ★ ★ ★

Chapter 29

(Late June)

The next morning Sam and new Marine Sergeant Tom Stafford sat in the Thompson Police Department's cafeteria sipping coffee. Morning roll call had been routine. Lieutenant Alban made his annual announcement that the Fourth of July weekend was fast approaching and volunteers for that night's shift were needed. The two wardens sat at their usual table awaiting police officer John Grey. According to Alban, the success of this investigation hung heavily on Grey's ability to recover, or as used in the technical sense, dust for fingerprints.

It was still early and Sam and Tom sat quietly without conversation. Sam sat so he could view the cafeteria's entrance. Finally, John Grey appeared in the doorway, "Sorry I'm late guys. Roll call went a little long because of assignments for the weekend of the Fourth. I escaped directing traffic at the town green … thanks to you guys." John looked at both wardens and smiled. Sam just nodded and Tom continued to stare into his coffee. John seemed an okay guy but the two wardens felt he was just extra baggage. They felt his presence was a constant reminder that their lieutenant thought them incapable of doing the job correctly.

Sam broke the awkwardness of the moment, "Yeah, okay … whatever, John. Look, we've been to this place a couple of times now. It's a little marina up river, hidden away in a lagoon on the east bank … and it seems to be kind of a wild place. There is a bar that is right next to the marina and also right on the water. We witnessed a near brawl there where one guy was thrown into the water violently. That's when one of the guys that had been in the suspect boat pulled out a bat to threaten the guys from the bar."

John's face reddened a little. Sam's demeanor and tone gave John the feeling that the warden felt he wasn't taking the assignment seriously. "Uhh, I'm sorry if …," Sam cut him off. "John, this is serious shit. If we have the right boat and the right guys, we're talking about killers … murderers. Guys that are okay with doing the deed and going on with their lives like nothing happened." John started again, "I realize …," Sam cut him short again, "You are going to be in as much danger as us … maybe more." Sam leaned toward John and stared into the police officer's face. "You are going to have to sneak in there with us, under the cover of darkness, and do your thing, without watching for the bad guys. Tom and I will have your back of course … we'll be watching over you, but if these are the guys that killed Hanks and they stumble onto us, we are going to have our hands full. I need you to be ready for anything." An embarrassed John Grey had stiffened and now sat bolt upright in his chair. "I got it Sam. I won't let you down." Sam nodded his head at John in an affirmative way and looked back down at the table.

Tom Stafford looked up from his coffee. "We will all have our specific responsibilities, John. Welcome to the team. It's Sam's baby so he's calling the shots. Just remember your place. We're going to watch over you like guards blocking for a quarterback on a football team. You will be armed, but your priority is to get the prints. Leave the violent stuff for us unless the whole thing turns to shit. Do you understand?" John nodded his head in affirmance and asked, "Okay, what's the plan?"

Sam began, "We're going out tonight at 10 PM, so go home and get some rest. When we get to the marina, we'll slide into a little, hidden cubby to keep the Carolina hidden … just like last time. When it's clear we'll lower our four man rubber raft over the bow and paddle across the lagoon to the dock area. That's when we are most vulnerable. There's probably around fifty boats moored there … all of them speedsters of one kind or another. Stealth is our biggest advantage. We have to get to the dock, find the suspect boat, get the information, and leave before anyone sees us. Tom's going to watch the bar and the adjoining shoreline while I get the registration info and the HIN number from the engine compartment. There should be a bat between the driver's seat and the inside of the starboard hull … dust it. Dust the helm …," John interrupted, "What's the helm?" Sam and Tom just looked at each other. Tom shrugged his shoulders and Sam stared at John. *Ah, whatever, he's not a sailor.* Tom offered, "It's the boat's steering wheel, John." Sam went back to laying out the plan. "Dust anything they might have touched in the boat … the throttle, steering wheel, and especially the bat. Those are priorities"

The plan now set, the three officers spent another hour discussing armament, equipment, and scheduling. It was agreed no uniforms would be worn. Just belt badges clipped to their trouser belts and dark clothing.

★ ★ ★ ★

CHAPTER 30

(Late June)

It was a typical mid–summer night. The sky was clear for the most part. Intermittent clouds passed overhead and a waning crescent moon presented itself. The night was a little humid disrupted by a slight but warm breeze every now and then. The mosquitoes were out in force.

Sam and Tom had arrived at the town boat launch and proceeded to get the Carolina ready for its night time spy mission on Speed Dreamers marina. The two marine officers had arrived an hour earlier than the agreed upon ten o'clock launch time. Tom checked the boat's equipment while Sam organized the night's equipment list. "We've got flashlights, paddles, rubber gloves, night vision binoculars, waterproof camera …, everything is here." Tom was in the bow and looked back at Sam, "Standard equipment accounted for. Lines, anchors, portable spot light, all good." "Did you happen to bring the mosquito net," Sam was hopeful. Tom reached under the raised bow and opened one of the hatches, "Right here, Skipper," and smiled. Sam smiled back. "Wasn't looking forward to another night of letting those mosquitoes drain my blood supply. We'll put it up over the bow and cockpit areas as soon as I park her in that little islet hideaway we had her in last time." Tom closed the hatch, "Sounds good."

Footsteps could be heard descending the wooden stairs from the upper parking lot to the lower launch area. "Here he comes," Tom said with a smirk. Sam looked at his watch. "Right on time too. Don't these cops know there is always prep to be done? I hope he's got all the necessary equipment. Alban will have a bird if we have to go up there again."

Officer John Grey walked onto the Carolina's dock and threw his duffel into the bow of the boat and smiled at the two wardens. "Evening gents. Nice night for a boat ride." Sam was the first to answer, "Hi John. Climb aboard. I want to have a quick briefing before we head up river."

★ ★ ★ ★

As John settled into his place in the Carolina, Sam began to go over the plan one more time. When he finished, he looked at each man and asked, "Any questions?" John raised his hand, "Yeah, I have one." Sam nodded his head, "Okay John, what is it?" John had a confused look about his face, "We're boarding a private vessel without the permission of the marina or the owner. Don't we need a search warrant?" Sam shook his head from side to side, "Nope. Marine officers have authority to stop, board and check boats … or to search … without warrant, upon probable cause that state or federal laws have been violated. In this case, we have reason to believe the boat in question is the Checkmate involved in a murder case of two years ago because of the driver's actions the last time we visited the marina." John nodded his head and said, "You are talking about the boat driver that attacked the guys from Joey's Speed Trap with a baseball bat the other night... right?" Sam nodded his head in affirmance. "Anything else?" No one answered so Sam continued. "Okay guys … remember to put on rubber gloves before you touch anything. We want to keep our prints out of the investigation. Less confusion."

Sam looked at his two crewmates. No one said a word so Sam went aft and stood behind the helm. "Okay, we're off then." Sam started the Carolina's engine and thumbed the tilt drive on the engine throttle to lower the prop into the dark water. "Tom, let go the bow line. John come aft and get ready to pull the stern line." John obediently positioned himself at the stern of the boat with his hand on the stern line ready to pull it from the dock's pier. As the Carolina's engine came to life, Sam gave the order, "lines away," and the Carolina caught the river's current but settled into a controlled departure as the 40 horse Honda engine bit into the river's fast moving water. Sam pulled the helm over to starboard and the Carolina was on her way to the Speed Dreamers marina.

★ ★ ★ ★

The Carolina sat quietly in the same little islet hideaway it had during the last visit to the Speed Dreamers marina. The bow pointed out toward the open lagoon where the speed boats sat silently at their moorings. The lagoon's water was smooth as glass since it was protected from the main river by a series of islets all of different sizes and configurations. Willow trees were in abundance around the lagoon and were one of the advantages in keeping the Carolina's bow hidden from view. Across the lagoon from the parked patrol boat laid the floating speed boats overshadowed by the marina's building and office area. Next to the marina's office was Joey's Speed Trap, a local hangout and bar where boaters liked to relax after a day of running up and down the river and spin tales about how they out ran the next speed boat or how they used their huge engine and superior driving skills to outmaneuver other fast boats.

The marina's office was dark and deserted, however Joey's Speed Trap was lit up like a holiday party and the Fourth of July was still a week away. Music played loudly accompanied by raucous laughter and loud talking. The officers took advantage of the noise and rowdiness to hide the Carolina. They placed the mosquito netting over most of the Carolina so that it draped over the sides of the white patrol boat. With the darkness and willow branches that draped themselves around the boat, the Carolina was now almost invisible. Occasionally, the gentle breeze that still accompanied them caused the willow branches to scrape along the sides of the parked patrol boat or catch in the mosquito netting but blended into the dark night as just some of the normal sounds that would be heard in such a setting.

The three officers sat in the boat just watching the situation. Tom was at his usual place on the raised deck in the bow and lay on his stomach watching through his binoculars, John Grey sat on a passenger's seat just forward of the cockpit's windscreen observing the party inside the bar, and Sam sat on the captain's bench seat behind the helm watching the dock area and the surrounding shore and buildings.

An hour passed since they had parked the Carolina in her hideaway across from the marina's docked boats. John was the first to break the silence, "They're making so much noise in that bar they'll never hear us splashing around out here when we start paddling over to that dock." Sam continued to watch the dock area, "It's going to be a slow, quiet paddle, John … deliberate strokes. Paddle in, paddle out … no thrashing. What they would hear is something different in the air than what is considered normal for the situation. You would be surprised at what sounds can stick out in the middle of all that racket. You won't be paddling though. Tom has the front of the raft, you'll be in the middle with all your equipment, and I'll be in the rear." John just nodded his head in a thoughtful way. "Just worry about collecting as much data as you can. We'll do the rest."

Another hour passed and Sam decided it was time to get across the lagoon and into the suspected lowrider. "Okay guys," Sam was talking low, just above a murmur. "It's time. No one has ventured out onto the shoreline. Party seems to be escalating if anything, so I don't think they're worried about the boats." He put his binoculars down and stood behind the helm. It had been agreed no uniforms would be worn tonight. Sam wore regular blue jeans and sneakers with a dark tee shirt. A baseball cap rested on his head and his belt badge was clipped to the right front of his belt buckle area. Also clipped to his belt was a folding buck knife and small mag lite. Both rode on his wide black belt at his back side. His .357 magnum was in its usual place tucked up under his right arm pit nestled in a high rider holster. The high rider was positioned on the belt so the revolver rode higher above the belt and was mostly concealed by the upper arm. Tom Stafford's apparel was the same except for his new Sergeant's badge that was clipped to the same place as Sam's. John Grey was dressed all in black. Instead of jeans he wore black cargo pants outfitted with several pockets of various sizes which made convenient places to carry his tools for dusting prints, his Maglite and rubber gloves.

Tom lowered the grey, four man rubber raft quietly into the dark, still water. The raft was colored a subdued grey so as to minimize any kind of reflection. Once the raft was in the water and stable, Tom followed and quietly slipped over the Carolina's bow into the now floating raft. Sam moved to John's position just forward of the Carolina's windscreen and kept watch on the dock and shoreline as John joined Tom in the raft. When John was settled and had situated his equipment, Sam lowered himself into the rear of the rubber boat and gently pushed it clear of the Carolina.

"Okay, Tom. Nice and easy. Slow deliberate strokes. Paddle blade in … paddle blade straight out. I'll match your cadence. Head for the end of the dock with the ladder … just like last time. John, stay low and keep your equipment dry."

Slowly, the little raft carried its three occupants across the dark lagoon. It was eerily quiet on the water. The slight breeze that had been present all night seemed nonexistent now and the dark dock seemed to loom over them with every stroke of the paddles. As they neared the dock area, new sounds entered the night air. Sounds of docked boats creaking and straining against their restraints while gently rubbing the wet, wooden dock. Above the lagoon, the party continued. It was the same noise, only closer.

★ ★ ★ ★

CHAPTER 31

(Late June)

The marina's dock slowly grew larger as the little raft made its way across the dark, still lagoon. It was a large dock consisting of two levels. The upper area, or deck was a continuation from a wide staircase that descended the sloped yard from the marina office. It seemed to serve as a viewing platform and boat preparation area. Six feet below the upper deck was the lower dock. It was a five foot wide walk around of the entire dock area and served as the mooring for all the docked boats in the marina. Access to the lower dock was from two points. There was a ladder on the lagoon side, at the far end of the upper deck, that dropped to the lower dock. The other access was directly from the shoreline that led to the gently sloping lawn toward Joey's Speed Trap restaurant and lounge.

The four man rubber raft glided across the lagoon's black water. Its hull had no light reflective qualities and served the little craft well especially for the job it was used for this night. The loud music and human noise emanating from the bar became louder with each dip of the paddles as the general sounds of the lagoon seemed to fade into the darkness. Tom Stafford scanned the area ahead and to the sides. It was very dark, compounded by the shade of the weeping willow trees that surrounded the enclosed body of water. The willows bent and although motionless in the calm summer night gave an illusion of long groping fingers that bent over and caressed the still water. At the top of the gentile sloping lawn, Joey's Speed Trap gave the impression of long windows of light encased in a black wall with human figures that moved about their interiors.

The raft slowly approached the pier that was outermost to the lagoon. The ladder that rose to the upper deck began to materialize. Just a few more feet and Tom would be able to grab one of the lower rungs to secure the raft. He stopped paddling as the raft slid up to the lower dock and nudged the mooring. Tom looked up the ladder that was now at the raft's starboard bow. In the dark, the ladder seemed much taller and the upper deck higher, but he remembered he was at water level and the shadows cast from the upper deck contorted most of the physical appearances.

Tom laid his paddle in the bottom of the rubber raft and reached out over the raft's bow. He found the bowline and secured it to the ladder that extended down into the water from the upper deck. Sam followed with one last stroke of the paddle and secured the stern of the raft to a pier that supported the lower dock.

Sam looked at his team, "Okay, guys listen up. Tom, I want you at the top of that ladder. Once you get there stay put and keep an eye on the buildings. You'll be our eyes and ears. No radios, no talking … just hand signals. John, stay by the raft until I signal for you. I'm going to sneak over to the Checkmate. It's the fourth one down on the right. When I get there I'll signal you. Make sure to stay in a crouch.

We will be in plain view of the bar's windows. Try to use the shadow from the upper deck as much as possible." Sam looked over at the bar then back to Tom and John, "Any questions?" No one answered. "Okay, Tom … Go." Tom grasped the ladder to the dock and climbed to the upper deck quickly and quietly. Sam watched Tom from his position in the stern of the raft. Tom got to the top of the ladder and scanned the area before climbing onto the platform. When he felt it was clear he eased his entire body over the edge of the platform and onto the deck, then knelt down next to the ladder. When he was comfortable, he pointed at the shoreline followed by a thumbs up. Sam pulled the raft close to the lower dock and murmured to John, "Okay, grab your stuff and get up on the walkway." John grabbed his equipment bag and climbed out of the raft. When John was kneeling on the walkway, Sam climbed out of the raft and made his way slowly to the Checkmate. When he got to the bow of the boat he knelt down and signaled John to come ahead. John duplicated Sam's efforts and knelt down next to him. Sam motioned to the Checkmate's cockpit, "Don't stop, just get in." John complied, tossed his gear bag into the boat and half rolled onto the passenger's deck chair leaving him in a squatting position between the two front seats.

Sam looked up at Tom who was watching the shoreline and buildings. Still all clear. Sam looked back at John in the cockpit to see he was busily organizing his equipment and familiarizing himself with the boat spaces they had discussed earlier. Satisfied, Sam headed for the walkway's entrance by the shoreline which was directly below the bar's viewing area. Minutes passed and Sam could see the top of John's head as he worked the inside of the Checkmate's cockpit.

John put his rubber gloves on and looked around the inside of the cockpit. He reached over to the far side of the driver's seat and found the baseball bat where Sam said it would be.

Quickly he set about dusting the bat for fingerprints. Once satisfied, John put the bat back and in the same orientation as he had found it. He followed suit with the helm and finished up with the throttle. John worked carefully and meticulously to ensure he collected a good set of fingerprints.

Sam glanced back at Tom who suddenly raised a closed fist in the air ... the signal to stop and hold. He pointed to a side door of the bar's patio area. Three drunken patrons were exiting and heading for the dock's direction. They were laughing and talking loudly but were still too far away for anyone to discern what they were saying. Sam stepped underneath the overhang of the upper deck and stood in the darkness. The three partiers began walking down the lawn toward the dock, stumbling and laughing as they went. Sam looked over at John in the Checkmate. If the partiers walked onto the dock John would be completely vulnerable. Finally, John looked up and Sam signaled him with both palms facing down. John's head disappeared back into the boat.

One of the men slipped on some wet moss as he neared the sand area and let out a painful cry. He rolled back and forth on the damp ground moaning and complaining, "Shit, I think I broke my ankle." The other two men just watched him a moment laughing and drinking beer. "I can't get up you assholes. It really hurts." The first man shook his head and said, "Aah, I didn't want to see your new boat anyway. Probably don't even have one." The second man reached down to help the injured man up, "C'mon asshole. You really know how to ruin a good time." There was a lot of commotion with colorful expletives and laughing as the two men struggled to get the injured man on his feet. The injured man was in pain and tried to make the other two understand his predicament. "Fuck you guys. Just get me back to the bar." Sam watched the three men with the injured man between them as they helped him back up the lawn.

Sam looked back up at Tom on the raised deck. Tom had his right hand in the air and twirled his hand in a counterclockwise direction. The signal meant all clear for now but to move out as soon as possible. Sam got over to the Checkmate as fast as he could and remembered to stay low. "Okay, John. Get back to the raft and be ready to move out. I have to get in there and get the HIN numbers."

John made his way back to the raft as Sam slipped over the Checkmate's gunnel and sat in the passenger's seat while he put on his rubber gloves. He moved over to the driver's seat and took out his mini Maglite making sure to keep the beam below the boat's console. Sam opened the glove box and frantically moved the mess of wrinkled papers and cigarette wrappers around until he saw a document that said Vessel Registration. He pulled out his small evidence camera and took pictures. The vessel registration included the HIN number as well as the original description of the boat, and previous owners. *Alright*, Sam thought to himself. *Now for the engine compartment.*

Cautiously, Sam looked to the upper deck where Tom kept watch. No change. He crawled to the Checkmate's stern and pulled the engine compartment cover off its frame. He turned his mag lite back on and saw the HIN stenciled on the right front corner of the inside of the compartment. Once again, Sam pulled out his evidence camera and took its picture. *Yes*, Sam smiled to himself. He slipped the camera back into his pants pocket and the mag lite into its sheath on his belt and placed the engine compartment cover back into it original position on the frame. Crawling back to the passenger's chair, Sam looked back at the shoreline, then back at Tom, and hopped out of the boat. Sam ran to the waiting rubber raft in a low crouch and slid over the stern gunnel into the back of the raft. Tom took one last look around and slipped down the ladder and into his place in the bow.

"Okay guys, lines away. We're out of here." Both Sam and Tom shoved the raft from the dark, wet dock and began their paddle back across the quiet lagoon. The raft disappeared into the night.

★ ★ ★ ★

CHAPTER 32

(Late June)

Sun shine began to spill over the ridge of the east hills. It was an orange red at first. The clouds that hovered there seemed to melt away as the rays became stronger and rose higher into the sky. Blue sky appeared to take the place of the white fog, light in color at first, then darker as the sun began to show itself. Sam watched the dim early morning sunrise from his favorite place on his cabin's porch. The bright rays from the sun burned and reached into the sky, until the whole airspace turned to orange, then bright yellow, only to be followed by a dark blue. The light transformation reminded him of when a camping lantern was lit off. The colors associated with the original burn were dark and angry but brightened and got lighter as the flame attained its natural size and shape.

Sam sipped his black coffee as he leaned against one of the porch posts. Traveller sat next to him, ever on guard, leaning into Sam's right leg. Sam spoke to Traveller, his gaze still on the sunrise, "That is beautiful, Trav. Look at those colors." Traveller wagged his tail in response and Sam smiled as he heard his tail thump against the floor boards. He knew Traveller was answering him. The coolness of the night was being replaced with a slight humidity. The cool dewy sensation on his skin was leaving and at almost the same time replaced by a warm moist feeling.

It was the beginning of a new July morning and a Friday at that. Fourth of July weekend was finally here, Sam's favorite holiday. There would be parades, picnics, swimming, and large family get togethers. It was the time of year for his favorite pass times ... sailing, canoeing cycling, fishing ... all wrapped up in one weekend. Sam looked down at Traveller and the dog looked up at him to meet his gaze. Sam nodded his head and decided he'd settle for this time of the year even though he realized it was also one of the busiest times of the year for a marine patrol officer. Any event he attended this weekend would most likely be interrupted with at least a phone call for advice on how to deodorize a pet that had just received an insult from an angry skunk to a boating accident of several varieties. Traveller wagged his tail again as if to say, 'everything is okay. I understand.'

Sam heard footsteps in the kitchen and knew Peg was up and moving around. "You're a good dog, Traveller. Let's go see Peg and get some breakfast."

★ ★ ★ ★

"Well you're up early this morning," Peg reached up and gave Sam a peck on the cheek. "Yeah. Couldn't get back to sleep so Traveller and I decided to get up and watch the sunrise." Peg smiled as she got to work on preparing the family's breakfast. "That's my Sam. The eternal naturalist." Sam sat down at the kitchen table and took another swallow from his coffee mug. Peg spoke to Sam as she worked at the stove. "Have you heard anything yet about those fingerprints you guys got from the boat the other night?" Sam replied without looking up from the table, "They've been submitted for investigation … shouldn't be long now. The HIN number I collected from the Checkmate's engine compartment was a hit on the original boat registration. The one from the glove compartment by the helm was a fake as was the display on the hull. That's the boat we're looking for alright." Peg smiled as she stirred the pancake batter, "How come the boat had two HIN numbers?" "I guess the bad guys thought they were being smart by putting a fake registration in the glove compartment in case they got stopped. Probably forgot about the one in the engine compartment which is permanently fixed to the inside."

Peg pored the batter into the frying pan, "Sam could you call the boys down? Pancakes will be ready in a minute." Sam called for the kids to come for breakfast. Peg continued to push the conversation, "Even if they find it's the same boat that was involved the night of Steve Hanks' murder how can you prove it was the same guys? There have probably been many people in that boat in the last couple of years. The bat with the fingerprints could have been picked up floating down river."

Sam smiled, "That driver just recently picked up that bat when he attacked those drunken patrons the night Tom and I surveilled them in the lagoon." Peg turned and looked at Sam, "So?" Sam raised his eyebrows, "So … the night of the murder … when Alban started to board their vessel … one of the two guys standing in front of the driver threw a life jacket at Alban to distract him. That's what caused Alban to fall backward into the Carolina." Peg still looked confused. Sam continued, "The lifejacket landed in the Carolina too … we kept it as evidence. If the driver handled that life jacket any time before that, and if the prints on the bat match the prints on the lifejacket, we've got him."

Peg was still doubtful, "But you said one of the other two guys threw the lifejacket at Alban." Sam nodded his head in affirmance, "That's right. But if we mention we have the lifejacket to him during his interrogation we may be able to get him to rat on the guy who threw it. If we find the boat was actually registered to the driver, the chances are pretty good that he would have handled that jacket at one time or another. Once we get a match on one of the suspects due to the prints those guys will be falling all over themselves to turn the others in.

The boys piled into the kitchen ready for breakfast. Peg turned to look at Sam, "Okay. I get it. Enough of that stuff for now," and brought the first batch of pancakes to the table.

★ ★ ★ ★

CHAPTER 33

(Early July)

It was Friday morning, July third … the day before the start of the big weekend. Sam Moody and Tom Stafford sat in the hallway outside of the Unit Commander's office waiting for Lieutenant Alban to invite them in for a debriefing and evidence results collected on the late night visit to the Speed Dreamer's lagoon. The two officer's sat bolt upright without saying a word. It was like sitting in a doctor's office trying to anticipate what was about to unfold. Finally, Tom turned to Sam and asked in a low tone, "Have you heard anything at all … anything from the lab boys?" Sam turned his head in Tom's direction, smirked and nodded in a negative fashion.

As if on cue, the door opened and Lieutenant Alban stepped from the doorway. "Good morning gentlemen, Come on in." Tom and Sam walked by Alban and into his office and stopped in front of his desk. There were two guest chairs awaiting them but the two officers knew better than to take a seat until Alban told them to. As usual, Alban closed the door and walked past the two men and stood before his window with his back to Tom and Sam. It was quiet.

No one spoke. Tom gave Sam a sideways glance and Sam just raised his eyebrows. Without turning around Alban said, "Take a seat gentlemen." The two officers obeyed and awaited the next step. Alban turned from the window and looked at his two marine patrol officers. He nodded his head up and down slightly then sat down at his desk.

"We have completed the investigation on the evidence you boys turned in earlier this week and the original HIN number had been changed. I guess they forgot about the one in the engine compartment that you took a picture of Sam. That alone makes that boat suspicious … however, the original HIN reflects the boat by the name of Streaker which is what Pat James saw as it drove past him that night. As far as the fingerprints go, John Grey did an excellent job. The prints all came out as identifiable and were compared to several prints on the lifejacket thrown from the Checkmate that night of Hanks murder. Some of those prints on that jacket are identical to the ones on the bat that Grey lifted the other night." Sam smiled and blurted out, "Yes!" Tom raised his right hand and the two men high fived each other, smiling. Alban cautioned the two officers. "Easy gentlemen. We're not there yet." Sam and Tom looked confused. Alban continued, "This is all circumstantial. The evidence alone will never stand up in court." The lieutenant paused a moment to let it all sink in. "We have the two year time factor to think about, the fact that we went in to a private marina … under the cover of darkness, and obtained personal information …" Sam cut in, "But LT, as marine patrol officers we reserve the right …" Now, Alban cut him off, "Yeah, yeah, I know all about the right to stop, board and search without warrant upon probable cause, but we went looking for the boat. It's not like they drove by you at high speed and reckless, while you were on marine patrol one day and caused you to question their actions." Tom Stafford stood up, "But sir, we've got them dead to

Dan Hayden

rights with the HIN and the prints." Alban shook his head from side to side, "Sit down, Mr. Stafford." Tom stood in amazement for a moment and resumed his seat. "Boys, we've got the goods on them but now it's about how we utilize the info we've gathered. As I said, the evidence alone is not enough."

Sam and Tom looked at each other as if all their hard work and time had been for nothing. It was a feeling of defeat. The murderer was still out there, running free and enjoying life and their buddy Steve Hanks lay in his grave un-avenged.

Alban saw the look and felt his officer's disappointment. He stood up from his desk and walked back to his window. After a moment, Alban said, "Gentlemen, we can still bring these guys in but there is still more work to do. It's dangerous and time consuming but it's what we need to do to bring these three men to justice." He turned and looked at Sam and Tom, "Remember, I want them as bad as you do."

★ ★ ★ ★

CHAPTER 34

(Early July)

"I can't believe we have to go back again," a forlorn looking Tom Stafford sat looking into his coffee cup. It was late morning and Tom and Sam had retreated to the Police Department's cafeteria to mull over Alban's suggestion. Sam was as disappointed as Tom. "Did you get a good look at the driver of the boat that first night in the lagoon … I mean after they roared into the marina and slammed into that other parked boat." Tom looked at Sam and raised his eyebrows, "It was really dark Sam. I got a look at him through the binoculars when he was on the dock threatening the other guys with the bat. He had that same hat on … like the one you described he wore the night of Hanks' murder … you know with the logo on the front and the palm trees on the back. He was clean cut looking, short dark hair, with a mustache … kind of slim, about 180 pounds, and around late twenties." Sam nodded as he listened to Tom's description, "Yeah, that's what I remember seeing the night of the murder two years ago. Other than Alban, I was closest to him before he went after Hanks. It's a pretty common description of a young man … except for the hat." Stafford looked up from his coffee, "Would you recognize him if you saw him?" Sam replied immediately, "Absolutely ... No question about it. I'll never forget that scene."

The two officers sat there a moment, not saying a word. Tom broke the silence, "Then you know what that means." Sam nodded, "Yup, we have to go to his hangout and talk to him. Tell him we have reason to believe he was involved in something a couple of years ago and see if he'll come in for questioning." Tom added, "What about his two buddies? Would you recognize them?" Sam thought a moment, "Yeah ... pretty sure I could. I remember thinking the whole scene was wrong that night and I never took my eyes off those three." "Then it's settled," Tom said. "When do you want to pay Joey's Speed Trap a visit?" Sam looked up at the ceiling and said, "We have to get Pat James in on this. Don't know what we're walking into ... going to need him for back up." Tom agreed, "I'll talk to Pat tonight ... see what his schedule is like and get back to you tomorrow." Sam nodded his head, "Tomorrow is the Fourth of July. There is a good chance they're going to be celebrating tomorrow night, especially after the fireworks. Might be a good time to drop in for a visit."

★ ★ ★ ★

The morning of the Fourth of July arrived as usual, sunny and hot. Fire crackers could be heard exploding in the distance already ... intermittent to start but with a promise of escalating as the day wore on. Sam rolled out of bed and made his way to the kitchen. He started to make preparations for a new pot of coffee when the phone rang, "Hey Sam, its Tom. Pat's in." A smile crossed Sam's face as he listed to Tom. "That's great, Tom. It could get a little messy in that bar once we approach that driver. He might just go off on us ... and if his buddies are there, they might want to join the party. It'll be good to have Pat's size there if nothing else." Tom's answer from the phone was an exuberant, "Agreed."

"Okay, we would have been on call tonight anyhow so I'll just tell Alban what is going down. I'm also going to ask for some unmarked police cruisers on the perimeter in case things get out of hand. We can't let these guys get away this time. We're leaving Joey's with them. I'll also give Alban descriptors (physical descriptions of the suspects) of the driver and his two henchmen so the cops will know who to look for." Tom's voice came back over the phone's receiver, "Are you going to have them in the bar too?" Sam replied, "No. We'll keep them in the cruisers near the bar's entrance and at the exits. They'll have to be watching the doors and listening for our radio calls." Tom had one more question, "Casual dress?" "Yeah, jeans and sneakers. We don't want to stick out ... belt badges under your shirts. See you in the parking lot around 10 PM ... right after the fireworks." Tom agreed and hung up so he could call Pat.

★ ★ ★ ★

Chapter 35

(Early July)

Sam sat in his white Ford Ranger pickup truck in the middle of the parking lot that served Joey's Speed Trap restaurant and bar. He had picked the spot purposely so as not to draw attention to his truck in the event any patrons that knew him saw it. He arrived a little early so he could watch the customer traffic in and out of the bar and the location of the entrance and exits from the parking lot and where they were in relation to the bar's exits.

The parking lot, like the lagoon, was bordered on all sides by weeping willow trees. There were some leafy bushes and swamp elms that filled in the gaps especially by the parking lot boundary furthest from the river. Right above the main entrance to the bar was the logo as described by Alban during his testimony after the accident. It read, Joey's Speed Trap, in bright gold letters, bordered on each end with weeping willow trees. The bar side of the restaurant had its own entrance and above it was a depiction of a scantily clad woman holding onto an upright pole extending from floor to ceiling with a logo beneath that read, At The Swamp. Sam grinned to himself. *Just like the hats they wore that night.*

The lot was dimly lit with a lantern outside the bar's main entrance and one makeshift streetlight near the bar's entrance. Placing unmarked cruisers around the perimeter looked like an easy task. *The cops are going to need night vision binoculars if we place them on the outskirts of this lot. They'll never be able to make a good identification from those positions with this amount of light.*

It was 9:55 PM. Sam watched as Tom Stafford pulled through the main entrance in his Jeep Wrangler. *That a'boy, Thomas. Don't park next to me.* Tom Stafford pulled into an empty space across the lot from Sam and remained in his jeep. Two more cars came into the parking lot with Fourth of July revelers playing loud music and shouting or singing out of their vehicles' open windows and parked as close to the bar as they could get. Sam looked at his watch. It was 10 PM, and as if on cue a huge blue pickup truck pulled into the parking lot. It was Pat James. Sam smirked and shook his head from side to side. *About time, Pat.*

Sam waited for the noisy partiers to get into the bar then got of his Ranger. When he got to the bar's entrance he stopped and looked back in the direction of Tom's jeep, turned and walked into the bar. Tom got Sam's message, exited his jeep and slowly walked to the bar and stopped as Sam had, and stood under the lantern for a minute. When he was sure Pat saw him, he too entered the bar. Pat James waited a few minutes and called Headquarters, "421 to Headquarters. We're in. Send the cavalry to park at the lot's perimeter. Tell them to stay in the shadows." Dispatch acknowledged, "Roger, 421. They're on the way." Pat shoved his radio into his back pocket, cracked his knuckles, and followed his two comrades into Joey's Speed Trap.

★ ★ ★ ★

CHAPTER 36

(Early July)

Officer Pat James passed through the foyer at the entrance of Joey's Speed Trap and stood nonchalantly as he scanned the room. The room was dim but illuminated in various places such as the band's staging area. Lighting was intermittent and staggered near the dining tables. A cursory glance to the left showed Sam at the far end of the bar with his back to the wall. A bottle of beer was on the bar in front of him. Tom Stafford had seated himself across the dining area facing the entrance and had a glass of something on his place setting. Pat looked to his right, saw an empty table near the dance floor and immediately occupied the space.

Sam saw Pat enter the bar and looked down at his watch. It was 10:05 PM. *Fireworks have been over for thirty minutes. We're only about a mile down river from the viewing area so anyone planning on visiting Joey's should be arriving any minute. It's not like they have to trailer their boats. They're just going to motor to the lagoon in front of Speed Dreamer's and dock up.* Sam looked over at Tom. He sat at his table, stoic, sipping a drink and watching the room of patrons. Over to his right, Pat was talking to a waitress probably ordering a beer that would never get to his mouth.

The minutes ticked by. Sam began to worry that maybe the fireworks party was not planned for this location this year. He glanced to the picture windows that looked out over the dark river. No lights yet, no engine noise. Another fifteen minutes passed and Sam caught Tom watching him from across the room. Tom raised his eyebrows as if to say, 'where is everyone.' Sam made no acknowledgement back.

Suddenly, almost without warning, the lagoon was full of engine noise and colored lights. Sam glanced out the picture windows from his seat at the end of the bar. Red and green running lights were all over the lagoon and more were pouring into the lagoon's entrance. The boats between the sets of running lights were invisible in the inky black darkness of the night but it seemed as if the lagoon was full and couldn't possibly accommodate any more.

Sam leaned his chair back until he felt his back was against the wall. *Should be anytime now. Probably tying up their boats and making their way up the lawn to the bar. Hope the three guys we're looking for are part of the crowd.*

Pat had his eyes on the main entrance. Sam and Tom continued to watch the activity build in the lounge area. The band was beginning to assemble as they rose from their tables and made their way to the staging area where their instruments awaited. The piped in music suddenly got louder and the bar activity was getting busier. Human voices outside Joey's were getting louder. Nothing discernable yet. Just a lot of shouting and laughing mixed with boat engine noise.

People began pouring into Joey's. It appeared some had already begun indulging before they ever entered the bar.

The noise inside Joey's was escalating very quickly. Guests came in twos and threes, and sometimes six at a time. Soon there was standing room only. Sam caught Pat's eye but Pat shook his head from side to side. The same answer came from Stafford across the room. The suspects had not arrived yet.

Sam got up from his place at the bar and walked out the side door that faced the lagoon. It looked like most of the boaters that pulled into the lagoon had already entered Joey's but there were still a few people lingering down at the dock area. A group of six men were standing on the upper deck next to where the suspect Checkmate was moored. There was pushing and shoving, accompanied by some laughter and associated expletives. Sam walked by the bar's windows so Stafford could see him. When he caught Tom's eye, he tilted his head to the lagoon. Tom slowly and calmly rose from his chair and walked to the main exit by way of Pat's position and gave Pat the same signal as he walked by. Pat waited for Tom to exit and also left the bar. When Pat was clear of the building he walked over by a trash compactor and pulled out his radio, "421 … all patrols. Party is in the lagoon. Stand by."

★ ★ ★ ★

Sam watched the group of men on the upper dock. They obviously knew one another and were throwing rocks out into the lagoon trying to see who could throw the farthest. Once in a while one of them would run down the stairs and gather more rocks from the beach to supply his inebriated friends. There was a dock lantern mounted near the ladder to the lower dock. It had been off until one of the men walked up to it and flipped a switch on its post, illuminating the end portion of the deck and ladder to the lower dock. "I'll show you how it's done," the man yelled, and proceeded to climb down the ladder. Sam snuck down to a willow tree that stood just before the deck and watched as the man jumped into the Checkmate and pulled a baseball bat from the cockpit. The man climbed back up to the upper deck and began taking practice swings. "Give me one of those rocks." He took a rock, tossed it gently into the air, and swung. The rock sailed out into the darkness. The group swore and laughed, "No fair." Another yelled, "that's cheating." Sam smiled to himself. *Now's my chance.*

The batter picked up another rock and sent it sailing into the darkness. Its trajectory was off and the sound of glass breaking in the darkness was evident. Sam took that opportunity to walk out onto the deck. All six men saw Sam appear from the shadow of the willow tree and stopped. The batter turned from the lagoon and watched as Sam approached, "Who the hell is that?" Sam made his approach obvious, "Hey, don't stop. Looks like fun." Sam got a good look at the batter now as he stood near the dock lantern. It looked like the Checkmate's driver. The hat was missing but the mustache, facial features, hair, and build all fit.

The batter let the tip of the bat rest on the deck as he held the end with his right hand. "This is a private party, pal. Why don't you just go on back up to the bar and have yourself a drink?" Sam walked up to the man, "Can I give it a shot? Just a little friendly competition." The other five men formed a semi-circle around Sam. The man with the bat suddenly smiled and said, "Sure … why not. You miss and we're gonna' send you for a swim."

While Sam was getting the group's attention, Tom and Pat had worked their way down to the dock. Tom was behind the same willow Sam had used and Pat was on the lower dock by the beach. Sam took the baseball bat from the batter, took a few practice swings, then let the bat fly out into the lagoon. He looked at the batter, "Oops … slipped." The batter started toward Sam, "You asshole." Tom shouted from the lawn side of the upper deck, fifteen feet away, "Hold it, pal." Everyone turned to see Tom standing in the lantern's light. Someone in the group said, "What's going on?" Pat took that opportunity and climbed up the ladder when their backs were turned and now stood between them and the water.

Pat announced his presence on the deck, "Gentlemen. Turn around and walk to the shoreline. We just want to have a talk." The batter spoke first, "Let's get these guys." Two from the group rushed Pat. Sam stuck his foot out and tripped one as he ran by and Pat just put his huge hand into the other man's face as he approached, stopping him dead in his tracks, then grabbed him by the back of the shirt and pants and threw him over the side of the deck into the lagoon ten feet below. Pat walked a few steps forward and stepped on the man's neck that Sam had tripped. "I can't breathe," the man could hardly get the words out. "Shut up … all of you. We can talk or we can play some more. Up to you." The group looked at the massive Pat James as he stood with one foot on their friend's neck, choking him. He looked like he could have handled the rest of them without moving. The batter spoke up, "Okay, okay. Let him up. What do you want to talk about?"

Sam stepped forward and unclipped his belt badge showing it to the group, "Thompson Fish and Game … We have reason to believe you were involved in a boating accident and we'd like you to come down to the Thompson Police Station to answer a few questions." "What now," the batter said. "Yup. We'll even give you a ride." The cruisers had pulled up to the edge of the parking lot on each side of

Joey's, overlooking the lagoon area. Pat had his radio out, "421 here, show your lights." Two cruisers on one side of Joey's and one on the other flipped on their headlights.

The batter looked at Sam, "Do we have a choice?" Sam just smiled and nodded his head in the direction of the cruisers.

★ ★ ★ ★

CHAPTER 37

(Early July)

Police Officer John Grey sat behind a table in a small room with no windows in a remote part of the Thompson Police Station. The room had one small light that hung from a string and pull switch in the center of the room. The walls were plain and undecorated and presented a cold, uncomfortable atmosphere. There was one other chair in the room across from John. It was for invited guests the police department needed to speak to about specific problems.

Across the table from Officer Grey sat suspected Hanks murderer, Bobby Sloan. Sloan was quiet and was staring at the wall to his right. Grey also sat silently, stoic to the situation, and waited for Sloan to say something. The presence of two people in a small enclosed room with an already suggested allegation, in dead silence, helped to create an atmosphere of awkward tension which was intentionally targeted at the guest. The intent was to put enough stress and pressure on the suspect to get him to start talking.

Grey raised his own coffee cup and brought it to his mouth. Sloan, still watching the wall blurted out, "Why am I here?"

Grey remained expressionless and said nothing. He merely stared at Sloan and offered no answer. Sloan's tone was escalating, "I was minding my own business … trying to enjoy the holiday, and you guys show up, accusing me of being involved in something." Grey remained silent, his eyes fixed on Sloan. Sloan tried to stand but Grey motioned for him to stay seated. Sloan glared at Grey, "Why don't you say something? Huh? You said you wanted to talk to me … I'm here. What do you want to know?

Grey remained calm and reached for his cup of coffee. Slowly he raised it to his mouth and took another gulp. He looked directly into Sloan's eyes, "Just want to talk, Bobby. Tell me about yourself." Sloan slammed the table with his fist, "No, you tell me why I'm here." Grey remained without emotion, "You tell me." Sloan looked back at Grey, "Tell you what? Tell you I was drunk and throwing stones in the water …," there was a pause. "Did that idiot whose boat I slammed into turn me in? He was parked right in front of me for cripes sake and it was dark. Yeah, I came in a little fast but he never gives my boat enough room." A few seconds of silence followed with Sloan staring at Grey. "That's what it is, isn't it? He turned me in … Didn't he?" Grey continued to keep his eyes on Sloan and said nothing. Then Grey tapped his fingers on the table, "Turned you in for what, Bobby?" Sloan looked back at Grey. His temper was beginning to flare again. "Cause I smashed into his boat a couple of weeks ago … that bastard … Told him I'd fix it." Grey looked at Sloan, "Fix what, Bobby?" Sloan seemed to calm a bit, "Aah, as I said … Came in a little fast one night and hit his boat. Caused some damage to the transom and the engine." Grey remained stoic and in an even tone asked, "How did he find out you hit his boat?" Sloan replied, "He was in the bar when it happened …," Grey interrupted, "The bar … you mean Joey's Speed Trap?" Sloan nodded his head, "Yeah. Anyway, guess he heard it. It made a hell of a loud noise." Grey nodded his head, "How did he know it was you that hit his boat?" "Oh, he had come out of the bar for a smoke and saw the two boats at weird angles to the dock, and us looking at the back of his boat … so he came down to the dock to check it out."

Grey nodded his head and offered, "He must have been pretty upset." Sloan nodded his head again, "Yeah, he was. Sonuvabitch shoved me … so I shoved him back. You know how it is." Grey didn't acknowledge. Sloan went on, "Then his buddies got involved … four on one … so I grabbed my bat and told them to back off or I'd smash them too." Grey leaned back in his chair, "You had a bat?" Sloan looked confused, "Yeah, I keep a baseball bat in my boat." Grey smiled, "A baseball bat in your boat?" Sloan sat up defiantly, "Yeah, that's not against the law." Grey sat upright again and wrote a note to himself, "No, it's not, Bobby."

★ ★ ★ ★

John Grey sat in front of Alban's desk with the office door closed. "Thanks for coming in at such a late hour, LT. Didn't expect you to be here at 1300 (1:00 AM regular time). Alban smiled, "I was expecting the call. In case you're wondering, it was me who suggested you for the interrogation end of this. I thought it prudent since it was your fingerprinting expertise that brought all this together. Thanks for coming in at such a late hour." John just shrugged his shoulders, "Of course."

Alban asked, "How is it going in there, John?" Grey smiled, "I think he's going to spill his guts. He is very defensive about everything." Alban tapped the desk top with his pencil, "Has he said anything about the night Hanks was killed?" "Nope. Just talked about threatening those four patrons from Joey's Speed Trap with the bat. Told me it's not illegal to keep a bat in the boat."

Alban smiled, "Did some research on this guy." Alban picked up some papers from the desk. "It seems he was quite the baseball player in college ... got passed up for the pros because of his temper. When things didn't go his way he was known to start smashing things. Busted up a few bars when he did try out for the big time, especially after a bad day of practice." John shrugged his shoulders, "So you think that's why he keeps a baseball bat in his boat?" Alban nodded, "Absolutely. The guy has had a major disappointment in life ... a very meaningful one at that, has a short temper ... and knows it, knows he has to let out that frustration or he can't stand himself, knows violence is the only thing that will satisfy that temper, and knows he's good with a bat ... may be some sort of a fetish. Whatever it is, he keeps it in the boat, has killed one of our rookies, scores of innocent fish, and who knows what else."

John Grey didn't know what to say. His job was to ask the leading questions without showing any emotion. He had just received a psychology lesson from the lieutenant and felt a little embarrassed. It wasn't his job to figure out why anyhow. John decided to let it go.

Alban saw the look on the police officer's face and decided to give him a reprieve. "John ... look, I don't want you to try to figure this guy out. He's obviously got some problems. Just lead him down the path to admit as to why we have all this evidence on him and continue the interrogation. How long has he been in there now?" John looked at the clock, "Couple of hours now." Alban stood up as he was about to dismiss John, "Okay, good. Stick your head in there ... tell him you're going to give him a forty-five minute break to gather his thoughts … get him a coffee or a Coke, and then go for the Hanks confession. We have enough to hold him on … even if it takes all night." John sat up straight and nodded back at the lieutenant. Alban motioned to the door, "Okay, John. Dismissed."

★ ★ ★ ★

CHAPTER 38

(Early July)

Officer John Grey followed Alban's suggestion and allowed suspect Bobby Sloan a forty-five minute break. He had returned to the little interrogation room for another go around and once again sat on the opposite side of the table from Sloan. Sloan looked tired and frazzled. It was two o'clock in the morning and aside from the questioning, Sloan had been out partying on the river all night. He lay forward on the table, his head resting on his folded arms.

"Okay, Bobby. Let's go. Sit up and clear your head. I brought another cup of coffee for you." Slowly, Sloan raised his head from the table, "Aww c'mon, man. More questions? I told you about the guy's boat. What more do you want?" Sloan shook his head from side to side and tried to clear his head. Grey remained expressionless, "Got a few more questions for you, Bobby. Then we'll let you out of here. You can sleep in one of the jail cells if you want." That got Sloan's attention, "Alright, alright, I'm awake." Grey waited a few moments then started, "You told me all about bumping into the parked boat at Speed Dreamers marina but can you remember anything else that you might have done to upset anyone ... something that happened on the river ... maybe?" Sloan looked at the ceiling then back at Grey, "Don't know where you're going with that ... told you what I remember." Grey tapped the table with his pencil, "You said you like to do the Fourth of July fireworks on the river every year. Anything stick out that might have been different?" Sloan didn't answer. Grey continued, "Did you ever have one of our marine patrol boats check you out? You know ... check your reg, safe boating certificate ... that kind of thing?" Sloan thought for a moment, "Well, there was this one time when one of those stupid marine patrol boats approached me and a couple of buddies ... night of the fireworks." Grey nodded his head, "That's not unusual ... right? Night of the Fourth ... people drinking. They probably do that to a lot of boats ... right?" Sloan just sat back in his chair and nodded his head from side to side. Grey leaned forward a bit and cocked his head to the right a little, "Why did they bother you? Did they say?" Sloan seemed to look off past Grey, "I don't even know how they saw us." "What do you mean, Bobby," Grey already knew the scenario and that they had anchored in a main waterway with no lights. Sloan continued, "Our boat was anchored and shut down ... no running lights on, no anchor light."

Grey sat back in his chair and let Sloan think about what he just said. "Bobby, you know that's against boating regulations ... right? Were you guys hiding from something?" Sloan was slow to answer, "Nah, we were smoking weed ... okay? You gonna' tack on another fine now?" Grey just smirked. "Tell me what happened next." Sloan recounted how the white patrol boat pulled up next to them and wanted to raft up. "The guy in charge ... the one doin' all the drivin' and talkin,' seemed pissed 'cause our anchor light was out. He's got these two other water cops holding the boats together and says he's gonna' board us. Imagine that? Didn't even ask!" Sloan leaned forward as if he was still shocked. Grey was taking notes, "Go on ... continue." "Well, I wasn't about to let no water cop board my boat so I told Josh to wait 'till he stepped on our gunnel and throw a lifejacket at him ... just to distract him ... ya' know?" Grey nodded his head. Sloan continued, "These guys really pissed me off. Hookin' up to me like that, coming aboard. Had my other buddy, Chris pull the anchor after the big cop fell back into his boat." Grey looked right into Sloan's eyes, "You said two other officers were holding the boats together. How did you get out of that?" Sloan smiled viciously, "Well one of those guys wasn't watchin' the show, so I pulled my bat out ... the one they threw in the lagoon on me tonight." Grey kept his eyes on his notepad lying on the desk as he wrote, "Then what?" Sloan matter of factly said, "Hey, I was the skipper ... had to defend my boat. These guys were gonna' bust me for drugs." Grey looked up at Sloan, "What did you do with the bat, Bobby?" Sloan was defensive. "I hit that water cop right across the back of his neck ... just to knock him into the water. Not hard ... just wanted to make him let go and fall into the water ... more diversion so I could get the hell out of there."

Grey was quiet for a few minutes. "You swear that all this is true, Bobby?" Sloan sat up straight in his chair, "Oh, yes sir. Remember that like it was yesterday." Grey held up the note paper he had been taking notes on, "Would you sign this paper I've been noting about your story to say that?" "Sure," Sloan took the pen from Grey and signed the confession.

Grey stood up from the desk. "Bobby Sloan, on behalf of the Town of Thompson, Connecticut and all affiliated offices, I am going to have to hold you for the murder of Officer Steven Hanks." Sloan started to stand but Grey put his hand on Sloan's shoulder for him to remain seated. "What do you mean murder? I just knocked him off the boat, throttled up and got the hell out of there." Sloan's eyes were incredulous. Grey remained standing, "You broke that officer's neck when you hit him … and then you fled the scene." Sloan started to panic, "You have no proof. No one else … except that boatload of water cops that saw me out there that night … and I had them pretty distracted."

Grey sat back down and leaned across the table, "Okay, Bobby let me tell you what we have. Grey pulled out a file of documents that lay on the table in front of him and began to list the evidence against the alleged murderer. "We have the prints on the lifejacket your pal Josh threw at Lieutenant Alban. Your prints were on that jacket as well as Josh's … and your prints match the prints on the baseball bat." Grey waited for a response from Sloan but the suspected killer sat speechless. Grey went on, "You kept saying it wasn't your boat but the original HIN number says it was registered to you." Grey paused a moment then said, "We found the fake reg in the boat's glove box, but you forgot to remove the HIN number in the engine compartment." Grey put the document back down on the table and looked at Sloan, "So in a nutshell, the prints on your boat's helm and throttle match the ones on the lifejacket … and the bat, so if I was you I'd get busy giving out some names."

Sloan sat back in his chair, "Didn't know I killed him," and then quickly looked at Grey. "How did you trace that to Speed Dreamers?" Grey stood up again as he called in the detectives, "Your hats, Bobby. The logos on your hats." Grey turned to walk out the door. Two detectives stood waiting, "Read him his rights boys."

★ ★ ★ ★

CHAPTER 39

(Early July)

The morning after Bobby Sloan's interrogation, Sam had risen early, anxious to get to the PD to find out what Sloan may have divulged. He left the cabin without even his usual coffee and quiet time on his porch. The trip to the PD seemed longer than usual and Sam found his foot was a little heavy on the gas pedal.

Sam pulled into the PD's parking lot, parked, and made straight for the lieutenant's office. Alban sat back in his big chair going through paperwork and photographs that lay askew about his desk. Sam knocked twice on the door jamb. Alban didn't even look up but kept reading, "Come." Sam entered the office, "Morning, LT. Just wondering how the interrogation went last night." Alban looked up at Sam, "Good morning, Sam. I've been expecting you. Close the door and have a seat."

Sam dropped into his usual place in front of the lieutenant's desk and sat bolt upright. After a moment, Alban rocked forward in his chair and looked Sam in the eyes. "We got him, Sam. He confessed and signed his name to it. Good work." Sam made a fist and cocked his right arm, "Yes!" Then he looked at Alban, "Who did the interrogation?" Alban leaned forward and put both arms on the desk in front of him, "I had Grey called in because he was the one who did all the prints and behind the scenes police work. He's also a trained interrogator and on his way to detective status." Sam nodded his head in agreement, "Good choice, LT. Don't want to have too many hands in the pot ... Right?" "Well, that wasn't really my reasoning but that works too. I know this was your case and you probably wanted to question this guy but you are too close to the situation. I went out on a limb letting you do the investigation." Alban paused momentarily, "In any case, Grey started with a broad line of questioning and slowly lead him back in time of two years using the information you dug up in your research."

Sam sat back in his chair and let out a sigh of relief, "He actually admitted it! I can't believe it." Alban smiled as he doodled on a pad of paper, "Actually Sam, Sloan never knew he had actually killed Hanks." Sam narrowed his eyes at the lieutenant, "I don't understand ... I was there ... YOU were there ... I saw him jump up onto the passenger's seat and come down with the bat on Hanks' neck. That was no accident!" Sam's voice became louder as he spoke. Alban raised his right hand in the air, "Relax, Sam. It seems that we had read his character profile correctly. He has a bad temper and is very defensive, especially when he knows he might be in the wrong. Seems as if he felt threatened when I tried to board ... and as he puts it ... without his permission ... and felt he had to defend his property." Sam looked confused and raised both hands to waist level with palms facing up, shaking his head back and forth. Alban continued, "He openly offered to Grey that once he caused the distraction with the PFD he threw at me, and the chaos that would cause, he meant to hit that cop only hard enough to knock him into the water which would secure his escape." Sam started to say something but Alban cut him off, "It doesn't matter what his intent was, or whether he knew what he did or not … he still killed a man and will pay for that. I think the fact that he didn't know the outcome of his actions led him to tell the story as he actually remembered it without further prodding from Grey."

Sam shifted in his chair and stared at Alban. The room was quiet for a minute. Alban looked up from his desk, "Do you have any more questions, Sam?" "Yes I do, LT. What about the other two passengers with Sloan that night? They were accomplices. Was there any effort to find out who they are and their whereabouts?" Alban tossed his pencil on the desk and smiled at Sam, "Yes. Grey was able to get their names during the confession as a part of the story as Sloan told it. The man who threw the PFD at me was Josh Taggart and the guy who pulled the anchor was Chris Jameson. Both guys had no priors … clean records … just regular guys out for a night on the river with Bobby Sloan. Detectives are on the case right now. Sloan came up with their whereabouts pretty quick. He was pretty scared once he caught on that he was involved in a murder case. Pretty routine. Misery loves company and once the accused is caught, usually spills his guts." Sam was in disbelief. They were going to get all the perpetrators. Alban went on, "Looks like they're all local boys. Detectives should have them here at the PD sometime today."

Sam was speechless. All that research and working between shifts. The night sorties up river with Tom Stafford and hours and hours of watching and waiting … the risks. It all finally paid off.

Alban stood from his chair and Sam rose with him. "You did a good job, Sam. You busted your ass on this one and I know most of that was for Hanks. Not that it'll bring him back or make his wife okay with what happened but it does bring closure for everyone." Alban reached across the desk and offered his huge right hand to shake Sam's. "Good job, Sam. I'm proud of you."

★ ★ ★ ★

CHAPTER 40

(Early July)

The remainder of the Fourth of July weekend passed without further incident. A notice was posted in police headquarters and mailboxes to all active Fish and Game officers to the effect that attendance at Monday morning's roll call was mandatory regardless of vacations, sick time, personal time, or change of shifts. All personnel are expected to be present.

Monday morning arrived as usual and the roll call room filled with game wardens, some bleary eyed and disgruntled, some ready for their shift, and some mildly inconvenienced because they were required to attend on their day off. The room slowly began to fill with wardens standing around and chatting, or making jokes. Some sat on the tables and discussed the outcome of Sunday's baseball game, and some just sat in their usual seat awaiting the inevitable meeting and its welcome ending.

A usual, Sam, Tom Stafford and Pat James sat in their usual corner in the rear of the room. No one spoke. Each of them sat and waited, comfortable with the fact that the three of them were present and able to enjoy whatever time they had together. Finally, Tom leaned over to Sam, "Mandatory meeting … think he's going to mention our bust Saturday night?" Sam nodded slowly, "Yeah, I think he'll mention it … probably use it as an inspirational speech to the rest of the unit … you know the 'and you could do this too' approach." Tom nodded his head in agreement with a thoughtful look. Sam looked at Tom and nodded in the direction of the opposite side of the room. Police officer John Grey entered the room and sat down. Tom and Sam looked at each other with raised eyebrows.

Right on time at 0800 hours, or 8:00 AM in civilian lingo, Unit Commander, Lieutenant Gene Alban entered the roll call room with his stack of papers and folders followed by Fish and Game Captain Fletcher. The room rose to greet the two superior officers only to be answered with an unemotional, "Sit."

When everyone was seated, Alban looked about the room. He noticed all the seats were occupied and began calling roll call. Attendance taken, he paused and shuffled some papers on the podium in front of him and started the meeting by addressing old business, which included department finances, equipment problems and proposed remedies, and open requisitions. The men were beginning to get drowsy as they had heard it all before. At least they weren't being reamed for something again. Alban went on to discuss department problems, most of which were of an internal nature and still not worthy of the officers' attention. Alban looked up and scanned the room as if looking for someone who had nodded off to sleep. Not finding anyone he graduated to the subject of 'change of shifts' and 'personnel assignments.' Finally, the lieutenant introduced new business. He cleared his throat and stepped away from the podium holding some of the papers he walked in with.

"Gentlemen, it is with the utmost pride and satisfaction that I am able to announce that the suspected murderer and accomplices involved with the Officer Steve Hanks homicide have been identified. The suspected murderer was brought in this weekend ... Saturday night around midnight and interrogated ... and has offered a confession."

A loud cheer went up in the room. People slapped each other on the arms and backs or playfully pushed one another in their seats. Alban waited for the noise and enthusiasm to wane, then began again, "It gives me great pride to say that this collar was due to the work of two of our wardens." He looked at the group and said, "Sergeant Tom Stafford and Marine Corporal Sam Moody." Alban stopped and looked over to the side of the room where Grey sat. "Officers Stafford and Moody were also assisted by police officer John Grey. When it finally got down to where I felt our boys had the goods on the bad guys I assigned Officer Grey to go in and dust for prints. Officer Grey was also responsible for the interrogations that night of confessed murderer Bobby Sloan." Alban stopped and nodded at the police officer, "Thank you, John. Well done." Once again the room broke into a round of applause and cheers.

Alban again waited for the enthusiasm to die down and let the officers have their moment. When the enthusiasm calmed, he went on to tell the story about the several night sorties the two officers performed under the cover of darkness for several weeks, the late hours they endured in addition to their normal responsibilities, the discomfort of the heat and mosquitoes that abounded the damp lagoon ... all required for the successful reconnoitering of the Speed Dreamers lagoon and Joey's Speed Trap restaurant and bar.

Alban stopped and looked about the room of officers. Their eyes were glued to the lieutenant, their faces now showing

Dan Hayden

seriousness and concern, as they too could someday be in the same position. "Gentlemen, after weeks of this, and secret meetings, it was decided to go to the bar where the suspects were known to frequent. Warden Pat James accompanied Stafford and Moody and went undercover as civilians to encounter the suspects and hopefully bring them in for questioning. As usual, on this sort of roundup, things didn't go as planned and the suspects never entered the bar but stayed out by the lagoon using the actual murder weapon to party some more. Our guys approached them and encouraged them to come in for questioning." Alban paused and smiled, "Of course the sudden appearance of several waiting police cruisers called in by James helped to make their decision. It turns out only one of those three suspects brought in Saturday night was involved in the Hanks murder of two years ago, but was the one who actually attacked Hanks with the bat."

Alban went on to explain the alleged murderer, Bobby Sloan, has come forward with the names and whereabouts of the other two men that were present in his boat the night of the murder. These two men ... who have since been brought in for questioning are being held as accessories.

The wardens were spellbound and looked about the room at one another sharing looks of surprise and satisfaction at the same time.

Alban waited for all the information to sink in and said, "Sergeant Tom Stafford, Warden Pat James, Marine Corporal Samuel Moody, and Police Officer John Grey ... front and center." The four officers left their seats and approached the lieutenant. They stood facing Alban and Fletcher with their left sides to the audience of wardens. Captain Fletcher approached Stafford, James, and Grey with certificates and medals for meritorious performance above the call of duty. He shook the officer's hands and said, "Well

202

done Gentlemen. Thank you. Please take your seats. Officer Moody please remain at attention."

Alban waited for Stafford, James, and Grey to be seated and turned back to the room of officers. "Gentlemen, as you know Sam's main responsibility for the past several months was marine patrol. He came to me one day and asked to reopen the Hanks investigation. I allowed it because of his new role and focus on the Unit. He researched the case, working between rescues and regular duty assignments, and led the entire investigation." Alban turned to the group, "Everyone on your feet and stand at attention." The officers complied. Alban turned back to Moody and stepped within arm's length of him. Alban raised his right arm and handed Sam his Sergeant stripes, the ones that were taken from him after the New Hampshire incident. Then Alban raised his arm in a salute and Sam returned it. Alban shook his hand, bent forward and said in Sam's ear, "I knew I'd be giving these back to you one day."

The room was reduced to good natured shouts and applause. Alban allowed the raucous nature for a bit then brought the room back to order and asked everyone to take their seats again. "As a formality, these stripes are a statement that Officer Samuel Moody is now reinstated as a full time warden in addition to his marine patrol responsibilities. Congratulations, Sergeant Moody. You did us proud."

Sam stood at the front of the room holding his Sergeant stripes and watched as the rest of the room erupted in jubilation. The men were out of their seats, slapping each other on the back, talking, laughing, and making jokes. The Unit had come back to life. Everyone was smiling and obviously enjoying each other. Hanks' death had been avenged.

★ ★ ★ ★

Sam watched the celebration. He knew that in the warden's eyes, Hank's murder had become a lost cause and had fallen in a crack like all the other unsolved murders … and worst of all, the bad guys got away with it. No one had ever talked about it but they all felt less than what they were because the very people they were supposed to guard nature and it's natural resources from, had taken one of the good guys … one of the wardens. Now because of the efforts of only a few determined officers, the Unit was now redeemed, at least in their own minds, and stood above evil and it's wrong doers once again.

As Sam's eyes wandered about the room, he noticed the quiet Captain Fletcher watching him. Fletcher had not moved from his spot behind the podium. When he caught Sam's eye, Fletcher gave the slightest hint of a smile and winked. It was the first of any kind of acknowledgement the captain had offered in the whole two and a half years Sam had been on the Unit.

Sam felt a warm, calm feeling wash over his whole being. It was partly a sense of satisfaction and partly a feeling of accomplishment, but mostly because he had fulfilled a promise he'd made to a fallen comrade a long time ago. Sam smiled and looked out the window. He murmured to himself, "Rest in peace Steven Hanks. We got those guys."

★ ★ ★ ★

Printed in the United States
By Bookmasters